THE New Year's BRIDE

KIT MORGAN

BESTSELLING AUTHOR

ANGEL CREEK PRESS

The New Year's Bride (Holiday Mail-Order Brides, Book Two)
by Kit Morgan

© 2013, 2014 Kit Morgan

Cover design by Angel Creek Press
Cover Design and Interior format by The Killion Group
http://thekilliongroupinc.com

DEDICATION

For my friend Gayle, who picked up the pieces at their source. Nothing like a Tackett to lift you up when you fall down. Love ya, girl!

OTHER TITLES IN THIS SERIES INCLUDE:

(Holiday Mail-Order Brides, Book Eleven)

A Mid-Summer's Mail-Order Bride
(Holiday Mail-Order Brides, Book Twelve)

For other books by Kit Morgan visit her website
at **www.authorkitmorgan.com**

ONE

New Orleans, December 1870

Elnora Barstow wasn't the most graceful thing in the world, but she wasn't a total klutz. Wouldn't you know, though, right when she needed her feet at their nimble best, they failed her.

"Run, Miss Elle!" Jethro cried as he shoved her into an alley and began to push her ahead of him at a rapid pace.

She stumbled down the alley only to trip and fall, the action toppling Jethro over like a mighty oak. He landed on the other side of her, and with lightning speed jumped to his feet. She didn't realize a man of his size could move so fast, and let out a gasp of shock when he grabbed her and pulled her up to stand before him. "We gotta move, Miss Elle! Dey be comin' round da corner any minute lookin' fo' ya!"

Elle looked up at her escort, and did her best to catch her breath. Not easy when you're frightened. "Surely we've lost them by now?"

Jethro, one of Mrs. Ridgley's two huge Negro servants, shook his head. "No, ma'am.

You don't know dis sort of men like I do. Now I gots to getcha to da train station an' on yo' way befo' dem devils finds us!"

"But Mrs. Ridgley assured me this wouldn't happen!"

"Dat was befo' dat devil-man Mr. Slade found out 'bout you! He done been snoopin' roun' da orphanage last few days, an' must've gotta look at ya somehow."

Elle's face fell. Mrs. Teeters, the head of the Winslow Orphanage, had warned her about a group of men who preyed upon the older orphan girls and tried to find when any of them were about to leave its safe confines. Having just turned eighteen a couple of weeks ago, it was time for Elle to either find decent work or a decent husband. Mrs. Teeters had strongly suggested skipping the first option, and pressed Elle to take the second: becoming a mail-order bride.

She took a deep breath. Option two was not supposed to involve running for one's life through the dark streets of New Orleans!

"Now don' be makin' no trouble for ol' Jethro, Miss Elle. We gots to be on our way!" He gave her another nudge to get her moving.

Elle was about to comment when a shot rang out. She spun at the sound, only to see Jethro, his face locked in pain, sinking to his knees. "*Run*, Miss Elle!"

She looked up. A man with a gun was standing at the other end of the alley, grinning like the devil as he made his way toward her. "Jethro!" she gasped in panic.

Jethro clutched at the left side of his chest, his face locked in a horrible grimace as he grappled with the gun belt at his side. "Why ain't you runnin'?" he said through gritted teeth. "You gots to *run*!"

She looked at the big Negro, her heart in her throat. The bullet had passed clean through, though it must have missed his heart or he'd already be dead. She knew that much. She also knew she couldn't leave him – if she did, he'd bleed to death. But she didn't have much time.

She dropped her satchel to the ground and looked at their assailant, who had stopped twenty feet away, gun still trained on the pair. He reached into the pocket of his jacket, pulled out a crisp linen handkerchief, and casually dabbed the sweat from his brow and the back of his neck as if he had all the time in the world. Then he grinned at her once more. "Come along now, and I'll let him live," he drawled in a deep bayou accent.

She turned to Jethro, horrified. "I can't let him kill you, Jethro. I can't!"

Jethro fell forward, just catching himself with one hand. He looked up at Elle with a face so agonized it tore her heart out. "You *gots* to *go*, Miss Elle," he rasped, his voice low. "Da train ticket's in my right pocket. Take it and run. He gonna kill me no matter what. Get me my gun …"

Elle's eyes locked on the gun belt at his side as Jethro pushed himself into a sitting position against a nearby brick wall. Blood oozed from his wound, soaking his shirt and vest.

"Whatever are you doin' talkin' with the likes o' him?" the man said casually. "Come, girl. Don't waste my time. Back away from him now."

Elle sighed as she pulled the train ticket from Jethro's vest pocket. Again she looked into his pain-filled eyes. "I'm so sorry," she whispered, and unholstered his gun for him.

"Run," Jethro rasped. "He won't shoot ya, ya ain't worth nothin' to 'im dead ..."

"I'm tired o' waitin'. Let's end this now," the man said with a sneer and began to stride toward them.

Elle saw how Jethro struggled to even reach out toward the gun in her hand ... and she didn't think, she only acted. Everything slowed until time stood still. Unthinking, she cocked the pistol, pointed it at her pursuer, squeezed the trigger ...

The shot was deafening, and she reeled back onto the hard ground. Ears ringing, she shook her own head and struggled to her knees.

Jethro sat against the wall, his head slumped to one side. "Jethro!"

He looked up at her. "Gimme dat gun, Miss Elle. Dat devil ain't gonna come after ya no mo', but ... dere might be mo' on da way ..."

Elle looked in horror at the man lying face down on the ground not feet away. "Oh my God, what have I done?" She looked desperately back to Jethro. "I killed him! Did I kill him? Oh ..."

"Gimme dat gun an' run, Miss Elle," Jethro said weakly.

Shouts could be heard heading for the alley. "Jethro! Someone's coming!" she hissed.

"Bad men, good men, don't know which. But run, Miss Elle. Either way, I ain't goin' nowheres."

Elle dropped the pistol in his lap and began to sob.

"Go. Do it fo' me..." Jethro closed his eyes and brought the gun to his chest, where he cocked it.

The shouts drew closer.

Elle let out a final sob, grabbed her satchel, got to her feet and ran. As she fled, she prayed like she'd never prayed before – for Jethro's life, and for her own. Would they be good men or bad? How could she know? If she heard one gunshot, that meant they'd finished off the gentle giant. If there was more, maybe he survived. But if there were none, would it mean they were good men tending to him, or bad men who'd found him already dead?

She continued to flee, stumbling her way toward the train station. She wondered if she would ever know.

She finally arrived, gasping and gagging for breath, and saw the conductor hop up into a car and shout his last call of "all aboard!" The train whistle sounded, and she made one final dash with the strength she had left.

A tall, thin gentleman stood on the platform near one of the train's open doors. He glanced at Elle before looking away, then did a quick double-take.

Panic filled her as she saw his eyes narrow.

She ran for the nearest car, threw her bag in and took a flying leap into it, only to bang her knee on one of the steps and go sprawling. She quickly looked over her shoulder and watched as the car moved past the man ... but he gave no pursuit, as if he wasn't sure of what to do. Then, neither did she – sigh in relief, or cry at the evening's horror?

She didn't get the chance to do either, as someone yanked her to her feet. "What do you think you're doing, running after the train like that? Are you trying to get yourself killed?"

Elle looked numbly up at the conductor's scowling face. "I'm ... I'm sorry, sir. I wasn't sure I was going to make it," she said between gasps.

"Are you all right?" he asked impatiently.

She nodded as she brushed off her skirt. "I think so." She checked her knee – no cut, just a bruise – then noticed he was eying her warily. "Yes, sir, I'm fine," she assured him.

He held out his hand. "Let's have a look at your ticket then."

A chill went up her spine. She looked at the ticket that was still crushed in her left hand and prayed there wasn't any blood on it – Jethro's or the other man's. Wouldn't that be tough to explain? She glanced quickly, and silently thanked the Lord when she saw it was clean of anything except her own sweat. She held it out to him. "Here you are, sir."

The conductor took it from her, read it and whistled. "Salt Lake City, eh? Long way to go – end of the line, in fact. Just where are you heading, miss?"

Elle finally let herself relax as she retrieved her satchel. "Nowhere, sir."

Nowhere, Washington Territory, New Year's Day 1871

"Spencer? Spencer! It's time to go – do hurry, dear!" Leona Riley called up the stairs. She stood in front of a mirror that hung in the front hall and adjusted her hat, then pulled on her gloves. "Where is that boy?" she remarked to herself.

"I'm coming, Ma!" Spencer Riley said as he stomped down the stairs to where she stood. "The stage isn't gonna be here for an hour. We have plenty of time ..."

"I know, but you can't be too careful," she replied as she inspected him. "Is that shirt clean?"

"For heaven's sake, Ma, I'm not ten years old! Of course my shirt is clean! My shoes are shined, my socks don't have any holes. I even polished the bullets in my revolver, if you must know."

Mrs. Riley's mouth opened in shock. "You did *what*?"

Spencer chuckled. "I'm kidding, Ma. Now let's go."

Mrs. Riley eyed her younger son and smirked. He was nervous, she could tell. She hoped she'd made the right decision when she took matters into her own hands a few months ago and came up with the brilliant idea of sending away for a mail-order bride for her elder son Clayton. Spencer had been all for it at the time, and played an integral part in pulling the whole thing off while keeping his big brother none the wiser. What Spencer hadn't known was that, not a week later, she'd sent away for *another* mail-order bride – this time for Spencer himself.

She'd delivered the news to him Christmas Day as his present – an envelope with a letter from his future bride and a marriage contract written up by The Ridgley Mail-Order Bride Service of New Orleans, Louisiana. He was shocked at what she'd done, but soon adjusted to the idea. He'd had no choice – his bride had already taken the train from New Orleans to Salt Lake, preparing to board a stage the day after Christmas to finish out the remainder of the journey.

She was arriving today, and Spencer was beside himself with worry. All he had was a letter from the girl, no picture. Likewise, she had no picture of him – only a small note written by his mother.

"How could you have done such a thing?" he'd lamented to his mother all through Christmas Day.

"Now, Spencer, it's for your own good! And besides, I'm sure she'll be beautiful! Just look at what a beautiful bride that Mrs. Ridgley sent Clayton! I'm sure she'll send you someone equally as pretty."

Spencer had still moaned and groaned over the prospect. And it hadn't taken long for the rest of Nowhere to catch wind of what was going on. Soon the whole town, already primed by Clayton's marriage, was abuzz with the news of another upcoming wedding.

Of course, many a pretty miss was crushed by the news. For years, Spencer had been considered the catch of Nowhere, but no one had caught his eye. Charlotte Davis had tried for as long as anyone could remember to nail Clayton down – before he'd married Sarah, and after her untimely death – and when he was wed she'd taken a run at Spencer, to his massive disinterest. Folks were speculating whether or not she'd have another go at Spencer now that Clayton was spoken for, but so far she'd given no indication of it.

Just as well, Spencer thought. He had enough to fret about. On top of his mother surprising him with a mail-order bride for New Year's instead of the new scarf and mittens he'd wanted (the usual tradition in the Riley household), Clayton had informed him he was stepping down as the town sheriff – and naming Spencer to replace him!

Spencer pinned the silver star to his vest, put on his coat and hat, then turned to his mother. "All right, let's go. But I still don't know if this is a good idea."

"Oh, Spencer – you'll love her, I'm sure! Just as Clayton loves Summer."

"I don't even know what she looks like."

"It didn't stop your brother." Mrs. Riley knew that would get a rise out of him – what younger sibling wants to be compared to the older one? "And she doesn't know what you look like either!"

"If we don't suit, I'm sending her back …"

"Clayton said the same thing. And she's still here, and your sister-in-law besides."

"But Summer is beautiful, both inside and out. I wouldn't have sent her back either!"

"But your brother is less agreeable than you are. It's a good thing he shot her when he did."

"Ma, don't say that! It's *not* a good thing he shot her at all!"

"Oh, stop fussing – I know it was an accident! But it did keep Summer around long enough for them to fall in love."

"Well, I think I'll keep my gun in its holster, thank you!" Spencer admonished as he helped his mother up into the wagon.

She eyed him as she took her seat and he hopped up next to her. "Of course you are, son. You'll just have to fall in love with her the good old-fashioned way. It'll take the time it takes."

Spencer gave the horses a good slap with the reins. "Ma, when are you going to stop romanticizing everything? What if love *doesn't* come in time? I'd like to at least get to know her first before I marry her." He suddenly looked at his mother, his brow furrowed. "You didn't make arrangements with the preacher for a wedding right away, I hope."

His mother suddenly became interested in the snow-covered landscape as they pulled out of the barnyard. "I do hope my asters come up well this spring."

"Mother," Spencer said in warning. "What have you done?"

"Well, you know that by the time the stage pulls into town, church services will be getting out."

Spencer pulled back on the reins and brought the wagon to a halt. "I am not getting married to someone right after they get off the stage! I have my limits, Mother!"

"Why not, dear? Other men do."

"Other men at least get to exchange letters with their intended before finally meeting them. I have *one* letter, in response to a note *you* wrote!"

"Her name is Miss Barstow, dear."

"I'm aware," he replied in frustration. "For another thing, *you* picked her out!"

"Actually, Mrs. Ridgley picked her out. But I have complete trust in her judgment." She crossed her arms over her chest. "Did you share any of this with Clayton? I know he hasn't been around much this last week, what with him retiring and you taking over the office."

"No, I hadn't thought about it up until now. Clayton's been too busy during the day … and just as busy at night."

His mother gasped. "Spencer!"

"Well, he *is* married now, Ma. What do you expect? Don't you want grandchildren?"

"Of course I do, but you don't have to talk about the details."

"You're the one that brought it up."

And on it went for the rest of their trip into town. Spencer loved his mother, loved her with all his heart, but to be honest, Leona Riley could be a trial at times. In a loving, motherly, I'm-going-to-do-what-I-think-is-best-for-you sort of way, but still a trial. This was definitely one of those times.

He'd tried to push the whole ordeal out of his mind the first few days by busying himself with making a list of his new duties as sheriff. Clayton wanted to get back to apple farming, and Spencer was all for it. He was also the logical choice to take Clayton's place.

But realizing why Clayton wanted to farm again – so he could be near his wife to keep her safe and sound – made Spencer wonder if he was doing the right thing. After all, if he got married, wouldn't he want to do the same thing? Then again, if his new wife turned out to be undesirable, maybe he would want to be away from home, taking advantage of a sheriff's long hours ...

He'd gone over it and over it in his mind for the last week: what he would do if he found his new bride to be less than he hoped for. What if she was a quiet, demure little thing that did whatever he asked? Would he be happy with that? What if she was cantankerous and argued a lot? Would he be able to show her what was what and who was boss in his house? What if he thought she was ugly as a troll and couldn't bear to share his bed? Even worse, what if *she* turned out to be beautiful beyond compare, but thought *he* was ugly as a troll and *wouldn't* share his bed?

He shuddered at the thought as he pulled into town, parked the wagon, set the brake and hopped to the frozen ground. He went around the wagon to help his mother climb down, and they went across the street to the sheriff's office.

Clayton was standing outside, and he shook Spencer's hand as his brother stepped up onto the boardwalk. "Are you ready for this?" he asked in a low tone.

Spencer took a deep breath. "As ready as I'll ever be."

Clayton let go a chuckle. "She'll be beautiful, you'll see."

"What if she's not? What if she's cranky and looks like a Guernsey?"

Clayton looked him right in the eye. "You can always send her back."

Then they heard it – the stage. "Oh, here it comes!" their mother cried.

The stage rolled into town and approached them at a good pace. The lead driver waved his hat at them as he pulled back on the reins and brought the team to a stop just past the sheriff's office. Spencer, Clayton, and their mother walked down the boardwalk as one of the drivers jumped down and went to open the door so the passengers could disembark.

Spencer stopped short and turned to his brother. "What am I doing? How could I have let Ma talk me into this?"

"This isn't the time for cold feet, Spence."

"But what if she hates me? What if I can't stand *her*?"

"Spencer …" Clayton groaned.

"What if she's covered in warts and hates little children?"

"Oh, for crying out loud!"

"What if she has a hidden past? What if she's *really* running from the law? Remember how you thought Summer might be?"

"Spencer!"

"What if …"

He never got to finish. Clayton grabbed him and spun him around to face the young woman just getting off the stage. "And what if that's her, you fall in love, and live happily ever after?" he hissed.

Spencer's mouth dropped open as he shook his head. "Things don't happen that way, but I suppose I could give it a try."

The woman looked up at him, her eyes wide, and mumbled something to herself before she said, "Excuse me, sir. I'm looking for a Spencer Riley. Do any of you know where I might find him?"

Spencer stood there, stunned into silence. This … this vision of loveliness was *her*?

Clayton rolled his eyes and gave his brother a nudge with his elbow.

Shaken out of his stupor, Spencer stepped forward. "Um … I'm Spencer Riley, ma'am."

She took a deep breath, smiled nervously and said, "Hello, Mr. Riley. I'm Elnora Barstow – your mail-order bride?"

TWO

Elle was indeed nervous – for good reason.

First of all was that, when she'd stepped off the stage, she found herself looking at the two handsomest men she'd ever seen! Did one of them belong to her? She certainly hoped so – she could already see herself getting lost in one of those pairs of green eyes, being enfolded in those muscular arms, burying her face in one of their chests ... *control yourself, Elnora!* she told herself.

But secondly – and it was a mighty big "but" – how could she possibly marry him? No matter how handsome and wonderful he was, he would be marrying *her*, and she'd shot a man! She didn't even know whether that man had lived or died, which meant she might be wanted back in Louisiana for murder. Nor did she know what had happened to poor Jethro – was *he* alive or dead? She had to find out what had happened after she fled – her whole life might hang in the balance!

Granted, if she hadn't taken Jethro's pistol and used it on her pursuer, her life would be in far worse shape. Jethro would certainly be dead now, and she most certainly wouldn't be standing next to a newly-arrived stage in the middle of the Washington Territory, ogling two good-looking specimens of manhood. But still, she was going to have to figure out how to handle the mess she'd gotten herself into.

Though maybe her husband-to-be could help. She took a closer look at the men and … oh, God, no! One of them was wearing a silver badge! A *sheriff*? No, no, no-no-no! Her intended *couldn't* be a sheriff! Or were neither of these men her groom? Were they in fact waiting for her because they'd gotten a wire from New Orleans saying a wanted fugitive was on her way to their little town, and they were here to bring her to justice? Murder was still a hanging offense in most places – she'd seen public executions back home. Had she fled all these miles, only to be strung up out here in the wilderness, or extradited back to Louisiana to face a sentence there?

Stop, stop, she scolded herself. She'd better find out what was going on before she let panic set in. "Excuse me, sir. I'm looking for a Spencer Riley. Do any of you know where I might find him?"

A few seconds of silence, and then the dreamier of the two dream men stepped forward. Unfortunately, it was also the one with the badge. "Um … I'm Spencer Riley, ma'am."

Oh, good Lord! It *was* him! *Stay calm, Elle. Just stay calm. You can do this.* She breathed deeply to still herself and tried her best to smile. "Hello, Mr. Riley. I'm Elnora Barstow – your mail-order bride?"

He looked down at her from the boardwalk, his face locked in disbelief.

Oh, dear. Had there been a wire, telling him what she'd done? He didn't seem to be acting like he was about to arrest her, but she didn't know how things worked out here in the West. Maybe he was giving her a chance to confess? Or just seeing if she'd wilt under the pressure? But if they found out, she would swing for sure! Her hand involuntarily went to her throat as she stared at the handsome – and perhaps deadly – lawman.

"Well, now, isn't this nice?" an older woman asked as she emerged from behind the two men. She wore a beautiful light blue dress and coat with a matching hat, and had a twinkle in her eye that lifted Elle's faltering spirit. If *she* was a deputy, Elle would be very surprised.

The woman went to a nearby set of stairs and stepped down to Elle. "Allow me to introduce myself, dear. I'm Mrs. Leona Riley – your new mother in-law!" She took Elle's hand and gave it a healthy shake. "Of course, that's Spencer up there, and next to him is my eldest son Clayton. He got married only last week, to a mail-order bride much like yourself!"

Elle stared at the woman. She spoke quickly, her eyes sparkling all the while. Her sons, on the other hand, were staring at her as if they were already mentally preparing the gallows. In fact, perhaps they ought to be after what had happened back in New Orleans. But what choice had she had? Was she supposed to let the man kill Jethro, and drag her off into virtual slavery?

Maybe, she thought, she should get out of this town. And the sooner, the better ...

Without taking his eyes off her, the elder Riley brother – Clayton – smacked Spencer in the back of the head.

"Ow!" escaped Spencer as he ducked away. "What?"

"Say something, you dumb bunny," Clayton whispered.

"Oh, yes. Right." Spencer cleared his throat. "Welcome to Nowhere, Miss Barstow." He jumped off the boardwalk and approached her as if he thought she might bolt if he came too close. Which, considering what she'd been pondering, might not have been far off.

With an effort of will, she held her ground, giving him a weak smile and a small curtsy. "Thank you."

The awkward silence returned for a moment before Mrs. Riley broke it. "What do you say we all get a bite to eat? I'm sure you're famished, my dear, and Hank's restaurant is right around the corner!"

"I am hungry," Elle replied. "That would be lovely."

"Then it's settled! We'll all go to Hank's and get acquainted!" Mrs. Riley said cheerily.

Elle looked in the woman's bright blue eyes and wondered if anything had ever dampened her spirit. Mrs. Riley's happy countenance and merry voice couldn't help but bring a smile to her tired face. And she needed some of that merriment right now. How was she going to get in touch with Mrs. Ridgley back in New Orleans to find out what happened? She had barely enough money to make it to her destination, and she'd hardly eaten a thing in two days …

At the thought of food her stomach rumbled fiercely.

"Oh dear!" Mrs. Riley exclaimed with a laugh. "We'd best get you fed right away!"

Spencer looked at her. "When did you eat last?" he asked flatly.

"Oh, I … well …" She didn't want to tell them she'd run out of money, and had survived most of the stagecoach trip on handouts and willpower. Jethro hadn't had the chance to give her what she needed to cover all of her traveling expenses. Given the circumstances, she'd been lucky to escape with the ticket and her skin!

Thankfully she'd saved a little from work she'd done at the orphanage – Mrs. Teeters had been having trouble making ends meet the last few years and had some of the older girls taking in laundry to help. She'd allowed them to keep a percentage for themselves, and Elle had saved her share all this time. She'd brought it with her in hopes of purchasing fabric to make a wedding dress. Unfortunately, she'd had to use most of it in the dining car of the train, and she'd spent the rest on food in Logan. If Spencer Riley found out she hadn't a cent to her name, wouldn't he start asking questions? And would those questions lead back to an alley in New Orleans?

"Well, I've been known to have a healthy appetite from time to time," she finally said. She watched Spencer's eyes dart to the hand she had at her waist, and she immediately removed it. She hadn't realized she'd put it over her stomach until he looked at it.

But instead of an interrogation, he offered her his arm. "Shall we?"

She smiled again and hooked her arm through his – just in time, as it turned out. Weakened by hunger, her legs suddenly gave way.

"Oh, my Lord!" Mrs. Riley exclaimed.

"Miss Barstow?" Spencer said with concern as he held her up by her arms. He quickly guided her to a nearby hitching post and leaned her against it, still gripping her elbows. "Are you all right?"

Elle got her feet under her and forced herself to stand straight, her face flushed red with embarrassment. "I'm terribly sorry, sir. I … I guess the long journey wore me out more than I thought."

Her stomach suddenly rumbled again, putting the lie to her statement. This time it was loud enough to attract the attention of a horse tied to the hitching post next to them. The animal looked her way, its ears pricked forward. How much more embarrassing could this day become?

But her rumbling tummy disturbing a horse was the least of her worries. She still had to find a way to contact Mrs. Ridgley and find out what had happened to Jethro and the other man. Otherwise, how could she marry Mr. Riley – *Sheriff* Riley – with a clear conscience?

"Would you rather go to the farm?" Elle

heard someone say. She looked around to see who had spoken. Good heavens, she'd better get some food in her before she fainted dead away!

"Miss Barstow?"

She looked directly at Spencer Riley. "I think I … I need food first." There was no more delicate way to put it. She could explain herself later, but she needed sustenance right now.

"Okay, then," Spencer said with a resigned tone. "Clayton, can you fetch Miss Barstow's bags?" He took her arm and wrapped it around his own once again, while Mrs. Riley – taking no chances – hooked the other one and guided her away from the hitching post.

"Sure," Clayton said as he stepped to the stage and picked up the one satchel the driver pointed to. "I'll just put this in the wagon and join you in a moment."

Spencer waved at him and pulled Elle closer, continuing on his way toward Hank's. "Are you sure you're all right?"

It was all Elle could do to keep one foot moving in front of the other. "After lunch, I'm sure I'll be right as rain," she managed. But her head began to swim, and she stumbled slightly against him.

He looked down at her, his face stern. "When was the last time you ate?"

She was getting a little annoyed – at him, at herself. "I think a better question is, when is the next time I *get* to eat something? Soon, I hope." She knew she wasn't making a very good impression on him, and tried her best to calm down.

"Stop fussing over her, Spencer," Mrs. Riley broke in. "Here we are." They entered the restaurant, the only one in town, and made for the nearest table.

An older gentleman came out from the kitchen and headed straight for them. "Well, well, I hear congratulations are in order," he chortled, then slapped Spencer on the back. "Come for an early lunch, eh, Sheriff?"

"Never mind about that, Hank. This young lady needs some soup, right now!"

Hank looked at the three, took in Elle's pallid face, and hopped to it. "Oh my! Right away, Sheriff!"

Spencer helped Elle to sit at the table, then took a chair beside her. No sooner had they all been seated Hank reappeared with a tray and three soup bowls on it. "I hope you like tomato. You didn't say what kind you wanted …"

"Just serve it, Hank. This poor dear needs to eat," Spencer told him as he watched Elle list to one side. He grabbed her arm and pulled her up straight.

"Oh, dear me …" she said as she began to lean the other way. She bumped into his shoulder and bounced slightly off it to straighten once again. But the smell of food was heaven, and she felt herself perk up. She looked at the bowls of soup on the table and her mouth watered.

Elle felt a spoon being shoved into her hand. "For God's sake, woman – eat it before you faint!"

She looked up into the concerned face of

Spencer Riley, who looked as if he was trying to decide between laughing out loud and force-feeding her. Oh, this was *not* how she planned on starting her new life here!

"Eat something, dear," Mrs. Riley told her in a placating voice. Elle swore the woman could make a funeral sound cheery. "It will make you feel better."

She dipped the spoon into the bowl, raised it to her lips, and tasted the divine ambrosia. The hot soup slid down her throat to her belly and warmed her to her toes. She hadn't realized how cold she was – she'd been too busy trying not to pass out! She took another bite, and another, and all too soon the soup was gone.

Spencer watched her the entire time, and as soon as she finished he pushed her bowl out of the way and slid his own in front of her. She didn't miss a beat, but kept spooning soup into her mouth. By the time she was done with that, their roast beef had arrived.

Elle found she couldn't stop eating. She was starved, and the food was appearing as fast as she could devour it. It wasn't until after her third portion of roast beef and mashed potatoes that she realized Spencer hadn't eaten a thing. He'd been moving food in front of her and watching as she wolfed it down.

How many days *had* it been since she'd last had a real meal? Logan, in the Utah Territory ... was that four days ago, or five? She couldn't remember.

And then it happened – the absolute worst thing in the world that could happen to a lady trying to make an impression on a handsome man. Not that she was even thinking about that – she was far too engrossed in the food. But when it did happen, she was still aghast.

She belched. Loudly.

Both hands flew to her mouth as Mrs. Riley gasped in shock. Other patrons in the restaurant stopped eating, stopped talking, stopped everything they were doing and stared at her.

Elle's eyes darted back and forth, taking in the scene she'd created. She then slowly lowered her hands, folded them primly in her lap, and looked up at Hank, the owner of the restaurant. "My compliments to the chef," she said with as much dignity as she could muster.

Spencer Riley looked at her, his eyes wide as his lips twitched. She wouldn't be surprised if he put her on the next stage and sent her packing after witnessing such abhorrent behavior, murder charge or no murder charge.

But that's not what her intended husband did. Instead, he laughed. And laughed. And laughed some more...

"Spencer, get a hold of yourself!" his mother scolded.

But Spencer couldn't. The last week had been too much for him – worrying about his new bride and his new responsibilities – and he needed the release. He'd worked himself up so much with thoughts of what kind of mail-order bride he'd see get off the stage, with whether he'd be able to be a lawman while fretting over the woman he'd leave at home. What would his mother do if he couldn't stand the bride she'd sent away for? What if he wanted to send her back? What if he kept her, but got shot by some outlaw and left her a widow?

But the second she'd descended from the stage, any thought of returning his mail-order bride flew right out of his mind.

She was beautiful. No. Not the right word. She *was* pretty, but there was so much more. He could see it in her eyes, though she was obviously worn out from her trip, and sense it in the way she held herself. There was determination in her eyes, a fighting spirit, as if no matter what, she was going to give everything she had to make things work. What man wouldn't want a woman with that kind of heart at his side?

Even when she'd faltered and almost went *down* at his side, she'd straightened up as soon as he'd been able to prop her up at the hitching post. He'd been prepared to lift her up and sit her on it while he held her to him if need be. It was sort of a pity it hadn't come to that ... now that he thought on it, it would have been rather nice ...

Spencer snorted one last time before he got his laughter under control. His new bride ate with gusto, and he discovered he liked it. She wasn't afraid to let him know what she needed, and seemed to be as upset about her current state, famished and faint, as he was. He was still determined to find out when was the last time she'd eaten – he knew his mother had sent plenty of money along for her to make the long journey west. Had she run into some sort of trouble along the way? Had she been robbed? But surely she would have told him so by now if she had.

"I'm sorry," he began on a chuckle as he remembered his manners. "I'm not laughing at you, really I'm not."

She smiled, blushing, and waved a hand in dismissal. "If it were me, I'm sure I'd be laughing too."

He looked into her eyes, which were much more alive now. The food had clearly done her good. "Have you had enough, or would you care to join me in a piece of pie?"

She delicately licked her lips and the action almost sent Spencer through the roof. He wasn't made of wood after all, and no matter how he argued with himself over this whole mail-order bride business, there was still a part of him that looked forward to the whole affair. He was a healthy vibrant male, full of life, strength, and … well, suffice to say he needed a wife! Better to marry than burn with passion, as the preachers said …

He took a deep breath to calm himself. "Hank! How about some pie?"

"Good heavens!" Mrs. Riley suddenly exclaimed. "Where on earth has Clayton been all this time? Didn't he say he'd join us?"

"He probably went back to the sheriff's office first. You know how he can't stay away." Spencer said, never once taking his eyes from his intended sitting next to him.

Mrs. Riley watched them and smiled. "No matter, I'm sure he'll eat something when we arrive home. Shall we be on our way?"

"After the pie," Spencer and Elle said, almost in unison. They both covered their mouths to keep from launching into hysterics and disturbing the restaurant again.

"Oh. Well, of course after the pie." No sooner had Mrs. Riley said it, Hank came back to the table with another tray, laden with a fresh apple pie and coffee. He laid it all out before them and Spencer watched as his bride-to-be looked at the dessert with a renewed gleam in her eye.

He couldn't hide the mischievous side of him any longer. "Tell me Miss Barstow, are you as good at cooking as you are at eating?"

She looked at him, her eyes aglow with something new. Had he insulted her? Did he just go too far? Maybe it was too soon to be teasing her …

Or maybe it wasn't. "Well, Mr. Riley, you'll just have to wait and find out. And if say I *am* as good at cooking as I am at eating… then aren't you the lucky one?"

Spencer's jaw dropped in a gaping smile as Miss Barstow dug into her pie. Yes indeed, The Ridgley Mail-Order Bride Service of New Orleans, Louisiana had certainly made a good choice for him as far as he was concerned!

THREE

Finished with their lunch, the three of them left Hank's and headed back to the wagon. Spencer was right – they found Clayton in front of the sheriff's office speaking with another man. He was tall, dark, and dashing in a farmboy sort of way, and Elle wondered how many other young men there were in Nowhere. Other girls would have to leave the orphanage. Would Mrs. Ridgley send them here?

"Spencer," Mrs. Riley began. "Who is that talking with Clayton?"

"I have no idea. I don't think I've seen him before. He must be a stranger in town."

Mrs. Riley peered at him a little closer. "I don't think he's a stranger. He looks familiar to me."

Spencer looked between his mother and the young man speaking with his brother. "Well, there's only one way to find out," he said as he made his way across the street to the pair.

"Come along, dear," Mrs. Riley told Elle. "Let's find out who it is."

Elle shrugged. Either way, she was sure *she*

didn't know the man, having just arrived in town herself.

"Ah, here he is!" Clayton said as Spencer hopped up onto the boardwalk. "*This* is Sheriff Riley."

The stranger looked at the two brothers. "Sheriff Hughes told me to report to Sheriff Riley. But I thought *you* were the sheriff," he said to Clayton.

"I gave it up – that's why Uncle Harlan sent you our way. My brother Spencer here is the newly-appointed sheriff in town. You'll work with him, not me."

The young man scratched the back of his head and looked Spencer over. "Well, if ya say so." He held his hand out. "Deputy Thomas Turner reportin' for duty, sir. Sheriff Hughes down at Clear Creek sent me – heard you were short-handed."

"Uncle Harlan sent you?" Spencer asked. "All the way up-here?"

"Harlan sent you a deputy?" Mrs. Riley chimed in. "Well, isn't that nice of him! I thought you looked familiar – I must have seen you the last time I went to visit my brother. What did you say your name was?"

"Thomas Turner, ma'am."

"Thomas Turner, Thomas Turner," she said to herself. "Oh yes, now I remember you! Your folks farm down that way. Isn't your mother Mabel?"

"Yes, ma'am," he replied with a smile.

Elle watched and listened as Mrs. Riley pulled the young man aside and got caught up on all the happenings in a town called Clear Creek, a few hundred miles south in Oregon. Harlan Hughes, her brother, was the sheriff there.

"We could have found a deputy here," Spencer told Clayton while their mother interrogated the young man for scraps of news and gossip from the other town.

"Well, you know how Uncle Harlan likes to help. Besides, this will give Charlotte Davis someone new to chase." Clayton smiled. "Maybe then she'll stay out of your hair and let you court Miss Barstow in peace for a few weeks. That is still your plan, isn't it?"

Spencer looked to Elle who could hear every word they said, but feigned interest in a horse across the street. "Yes, that's my plan. Convincing Ma of that is another story. If she had her way, she'd have us married this afternoon."

Clayton glanced to Elle, than slapped him on the back. "Would that be so bad?"

Spencer rolled his eyes at his brother, left Thomas Turner to deal with his mother's long string of questions, and went to stand next to Elle. "Are you feeling better now?"

"Oh yes, quite. Lunch was lovely."

"Yes, all three courses."

She looked at him, puzzled. "Courses?"

"Soup, the roast beef, dessert … you know. Courses."

The truth was, she *didn't* know – growing up in an orphanage didn't exactly educate her much on fancy dining. She smiled weakly and nodded.

She had an awful lot to learn.

Which reminded her. "Do you have a telegraph office in town?" she asked.

"Yes, why?"

"I … wanted to let Mrs. Ridgley know I've arrived safely."

"Oh, of course. But we can take care of that later. I'd like to see you home to the farm if you don't mind. It looks like I'll need to come back into town and get Mr. Turner settled."

She watched as Mrs. Riley grabbed the young man's arm and dragged him back to where they stood. "Oh, it's just too wonderful – the stories this young man has to tell!"

"Ma, we haven't time. I need to take you home now," Spencer told her.

"Oh, but Mr. Turner has been telling me all about Clear Creek!" She turned to Elle. "They have some very interesting folks living down there in that little town."

"Not now, Ma. Another time perhaps." Spencer gave his attention to Mr. Turner. "I need to take the women home, but I'll be back and we can talk about your position then."

"Yes, sir." Thomas Turner said. He then turned to Elle and Mrs. Riley, tipped his hat, and followed Clayton inside the sheriff's office.

"Isn't Clayton coming?" Mrs. Riley asked.

"He'll have Mr. Turner fill out some paperwork, then come home about the time I have to come back. Don't worry, Ma, I'll return in time for supper."

"Oh, but Spencer, do you have to work this afternoon? Miss Barstow just got here."

"Ma – don't worry! Let's give her a chance to settle in, get the run of the place while I get other things out of my hair. Then I can come home and try some of Miss Barstow's cooking. Maybe then she'll tell me how she came to town with such an unnaturally healthy appetite." He winked at her.

Elle blushed. He probably still wanted to know what happened to the money he'd sent Mrs. Ridgley. But could she trust him enough to tell him what had happened? Would he lock her up in jail the moment he found out? Best to wait to hear from Mrs. Ridgley first, then she'd do what she had to do. Whatever that was.

"I'm sure the last thing on Miss Barstow's mind is cooking. She'll need to rest after such a long journey. Besides, Summer will have supper prepared in no time."

Elle perked up. "Summer?"

"Yes, dear. Summer is Clayton's wife."

Elle's eyes widened. Could it be? "Summer James?" she blurted.

"Why, yes! But it's Summer Riley now, of cour–"

"Oh, my Lord!" Elle cried as both hands flew to her mouth. "Summer!" She quickly turned and, in a very unladylike move, leapt down the stairs of the boardwalk and ran for the wagon.

"Oh dear!" Mrs. Riley said. "Did she just do what I think she did?"

"Well … yes, of course she did," Spencer replied, confused. "I mean, we both just watched her do it, didn't we?"

"Spencer, that is not what I … oh, never

mind," his mother said as she lifted her skirts and made her way down the steps to the street.

Spencer watched her go, then saw Miss Barstow climb onto the wagon without any help. *What got into her?* he wondered.

"My, my," a voice cooed from behind him. "Somebody's bride is certainly in a hurry to get home."

Spencer stiffened in annoyance, sighed, then turned and looked into the preening face of Charlotte Davis. "Good afternoon, Miss Davis," he said flatly. Darned if he was going to be rude, but darned if he was going to let this preening, flirting busybody – who'd tried so hard to wreck his brother's engagement to Summer – feel welcome, either.

Charlotte didn't seem to notice his coldness. "Better hurry on home, Spencer. She looks like she's ready to bust a gut, she's so excited."

"In fact," Spencer replied, "I think I might just do that." *If only to get myself – and Miss Barstow – away from you*, he didn't add.

"Do give my best to your brother," she purred.

"I shall." Spencer kept his eyes focused on her, fearful of giving away that Clayton was just behind her inside the sheriff's office. Everyone knew Charlotte still had it bad for Clayton. It didn't even seem to matter to her he was now married – she still flirted with him every chance she got. Granted, Charlotte flirted with everyone, but Clayton got more than the usual share.

He suddenly felt sorry for the new deputy.

Poor Thomas Turner had no idea what was coming once Charlotte set eyes on *him*.

"Good day, ma'am." Spencer tipped his hat, hopped off the boardwalk and hurried across the street to the wagon. He had more important things to worry about than Charlotte Davis. For one, why had his future bride just run off the boardwalk and climbed up onto the wagon like she was escaping a fire? Why did she get so excited about Clayton's wife Summer all of a sudden? Did they know each other? And what other sorts of surprises did his future bride have in store for him?

Well, he supposed he was about to find out …

No sooner had they gotten home and out of the wagon that Spencer heard a call from the porch. "Elle?"

"Summer!" With her eyes lit up like lightning bugs, Elle launched herself at Summer Riley.

"Careful!" Spencer cried as he grabbed Elle's arm to keep her from toppling them both over. "Summer's had an injury!"

"Oh!" Elle exclaimed, then looked Summer over more carefully. "I'm sorry, I didn't know!"

"Are you always this excitable?" Spencer asked as he shoved his hat off his forehead in relief.

"I'm sorry, Mr. Riley. It's just that …"

"Elle and I have known each other from childhood," Summer finished for her, then threw her arms around her friend. "Oh, how I've missed you!" She let go of Elle and pulled back to study her. "Mrs. Teeters?"

Elle smiled. "She's well, and crankier than ever."

"And the others – what of the others?"

"Which group?"

Summer's smile faded. "Ours."

Elle glanced to Spencer, then back to Summer. "I'll tell you just as soon as I'm settled. And I want to hear all about your husband, the wedding, everything!"

Summer's face brightened. "All right, I'll show you to your room." With a swish of skirts Summer turned and limped into the house and down the hall.

"What happened?" Elle asked as she followed her, Spencer on her heels.

Summer stopped in front of a door at the end of the hall. "It's nothing, really."

"Nothing?" Spencer quipped. "You call being shot nothing?"

"Shot?" Elle squeaked.

"Spencer, let's not upset Elle. She's just arrived," Summer told him calmly.

"You were shot?" Elle asked again.

"It was an accident." Summer and Spencer said in unison.

Elle looked between the two, her attention finally settling on Summer. "Who on earth shot you?"

"Clayton," she answered with a sigh, opened

the door and went into the room.

"Wait! You were shot by your husband?!?" Elle's voice had risen an entire octave.

"It was an *accident*!" Spencer repeated, his own voice going up.

"Let's not talk about it anymore right now. I'll explain later," Summer said. "Right now you should rest. I remember what a long, exhausting journey it was coming out here from New Orleans."

Elle looked at her and their eyes locked. She swallowed. "Yes … it was exhausting. I could do with a few moments to myself."

"Are you hungry?" Summer asked. "Can I fix you anything?"

Spencer began to chuckle.

Elle smiled again, resisting the urge to glare at him. "I'm fine." She was still going to have to explain, but first things first – she really did need to rest. Between the long trip and the huge meal, she was incredibly tired.

Besides, she didn't relish facing Spencer Riley or even Summer when the questioning started. And they *would* have questions, both of them. Spencer would ask why she ran out of money during her long journey. Summer would ask about the other orphans – had any of them been adopted, who was next to leave … had she had any trouble getting out …

Summer had spoken to her before she'd embarked on her own journey west, and had mentioned the man called Mr. Slade and what his kind did with girls from the orphanage if they could get their hands on them. Mrs.

Ridgley was trying to make sure such girls had an alternative to the streets of the Crescent City. Jobs were scarce there, and protection from the likes of Mr. Slade practically non-existent. Too many of their lot had already fallen victim to the brothels and underground slave blocks thanks to men just like him.

But Elle had a bigger problem. She'd left Mr. Slade behind in New Orleans … but had she also left behind a dead man? And if so, was it only a matter of time before the law caught up to her? Would it be better if she turned herself in? Of course, the only problem with that was, she was supposed to marry the very man she'd have to turn herself in to ...

"Elle?" Summer asked. "Are you all right? You look awfully pale."

Elle swallowed and sank onto the bed. "I'll be fine … just tired, is all." "Tired" was an understatement, and paled next to "scared out of her wits". She looked up at Spencer, who was staring down at her, his face blank, as if she was just another detail to deal with that day. What would he do if she told him? Even if the man in New Orleans lived, would the sheriff of Nowhere still want to marry her knowing she'd shot someone? Even in self-defense?

She'd gone over it a thousand times in her head during her journey. She was sure it could be called self-defense. But without any witnesses, Mr. Slade's man (if he'd survived) could call it something else entirely. Who would a jury believe, a poor orphan girl or a (seeming) gentleman? And what of Jethro – was *he* still alive?

"Do you want some water at least?" Summer asked, still concerned. "I can get some for you."

Elle looked up at her and barely nodded in answer. Her mind was full of the horrific ordeal that had sent her running for her life. It seemed so long ago, but it hadn't even been two weeks ...

"Here's your bag. This is all you brought with you?" Spencer asked, his eyes now filled with something Elle hadn't noticed before.

She looked at him and felt the fear in her heart subside. For a moment she couldn't speak, but finally said, "Yes, that's all. I should rest now."

"Okay, monkey. You do that."

She looked at him again, "What did you say?"

He smiled. "Monkey."

"What … what is that supposed to mean?"

He chuckled again. "I saw the way you scrambled up onto the wagon. I had no idea you and Summer knew each other, but now I understand why you got so excited. You reminded me of a monkey when you took off the way you did and climbed up without any help."

"Oh, that," Elle said as she flushed with embarrassment. "I suppose that wasn't very ladylike of me, was it?"

"Mmm, maybe not. Mother is still in shock. She went straight upstairs, probably to write letters to our other relatives to let them know you've arrived."

"And tell them I'm a monkey?"

He smiled. "No. That's my name for you."

Summer shook her head. "Let her get some rest," she scolded, then turned back to Elle. "You'll have to get used to the Rileys' sense of humor. It takes a while."

Elle smiled and took one of Summer's hands in her own. "I'm glad I've found you again. It's more than I could have hoped for."

Summer sat on the bed and hugged her. "I've been blessed with a wonderful husband, a new family, and now my best friend. Life couldn't be more perfect than it is right now. I'm so glad you're here."

Elle felt the hot sting of tears threaten. "Me, too."

The only question was, how long would she be there to enjoy it?

FOUR

Sleep didn't come as easily as Elle had hoped. Her mind was spinning with thoughts of being thrown into jail by Spencer Riley, of Summer's horrified expression when she told her what happened, of the look of utter disappointment on Mrs. Riley's face to find the mail-order bride she'd sent away for turned out to be a wanted fugitive ...

... that is, if they ever found out.

And Elle was more determined than ever that they wouldn't – at least not until she herself knew what had happened. Tomorrow, she'd ask Spencer to take her to town to wire Mrs. Ridgley. Within a few days she was sure she'd have an answer. Only once that happened would she worry about what to do next. But for now, she had to put it out of her mind. As it was, she hadn't gotten any sleep – she hoped she wouldn't be poor company when it came time for dinner.

Already she could smell chicken frying and biscuits baking in the oven. She decided that if she wasn't going to nap, she should at least get up and help Summer prepare the meal, especially since the poor girl had an injured foot. Now *that* story she had to hear!

She found her friend at the stove poking into a pot of boiling potatoes. "Can I help?"

Summer jumped. "Oh! My goodness, I didn't hear you come up behind me! I forgot how quiet you are on your feet."

Elle smiled and shrugged. "Sorry. I guess I'm so used to tip-toeing around the orphanage that it's a hard habit to break."

Summer laughed. "You never know when it'll come in handy around here. It might be fun to pull a few pranks on Clayton and Spencer."

"Oh, I don't know about that …," Elle said nervously.

"Don't worry, we'll wait until after you and Spencer are married."

Elle said nothing immediately in response. *Would* they ever get married? She honestly didn't know, given what she'd left behind. And on the chance they did … "Tell me about him. About Spencer."

"You didn't get a letter from him?"

"No, only a short note he added when he answered the advertisement."

Summer turned from her and took a couple of dishrags from the worktable. "Oh, that. Well …"

"If he did send along another letter I never got it. Mrs. Ridgley told me she contacted Mrs. Teeters about Mr. Riley's application the same day she received it. Mrs. Teeters said I could have a little time to decide what I wanted to do.

I liked what he wrote in his note, though. The very next day Mrs. Teeters insisted I head out here, and I figured if it was good enough for you then it was good enough for me. So I wrote Mr. Riley a letter telling him about myself, and Mrs. Ridgley sent it off with the contract. And here I am."

Summer closed her eyes and gripped the back of one of the kitchen chairs. "Things are worse than when I left."

"I know Mrs. Teeters didn't give me a chance to find a job, like she did you."

Summer nodded solemnly. "That's because she knows there are none to be found." She grabbed Elle to her in a fierce hug. "Thank the Lord Spencer was the one to answer that advertisement! If he hadn't, and some other man had, God only knows where you might have ended up!"

"And we never would have seen each other again …," Elle added, her voice trailing off. In fact, the more she thought about everything, even with what happened when she left, finding Summer again was a pure miracle!

Elle wrapped Summer in her arms. "I shall thank the Lord daily for this!" she whispered before backing away.

"As will I," Summer said, wiping a tear from her eye. "Now let's see to dinner. The men will be hungry when they return home."

"Isn't Clayton already home?"

"No. Spencer left shortly after you lay down. I've not seen either one of them since. Mother should be down soon – she's upstairs writing letters."

"Still?"

"Your arrival is big news. She did the same thing when I arrived, only I didn't realize it. I was too busy trying to figure out how to walk."

"Oh, yes, your foot. How did that happen?"

Summer laughed. "Clayton shot me right after I got off the stage."

"Oh, good Lord!"

Summer laughed again as she picked up a folded dishrag and opened the oven. "It really was an accident, though. It's quite funny now, but it certainly wasn't at the time." She took out the biscuits and set the pan on the nearby worktable. "Suffice to say, if he hadn't shot me, I might not still be here."

Elle could only smile. "Oh, I can't wait to hear this."

"I'll tell you all about it when we have more time, and I'm sure you'll be beside yourself with laughter. In the meantime, help me with the potatoes, will you?"

Elle helped Summer finish preparing the evening meal. She was worried the men wouldn't be home in time to eat while the food was hot, but no sooner did they have everything ready than Spencer and Clayton came through the front door.

And they weren't alone. "Oh, what a delightful surprise!" Mrs. Riley exclaimed as she came down the stairs. "Mr. Turner!"

Thomas Turner smiled at her and removed his hat. "Evening, ma'am."

"We thought Mr. Turner could do with a

home-cooked meal," Spencer told her. "We've arranged for him to stay out at the Blakes' until he gets a place of his own."

Summer and Elle came down the hall to greet them. Elle almost flinched at the pinch of envy she felt when Clayton took Summer in his arms, kissed her on the cheek, and whispered in her ear. She stole a glance at Spencer, but he was busy hanging up his coat. Just as well – she might never know what it was like to be embraced so warmly and kissed, nor have a handsome man speak secrets to her. She was the one with the secret, not Spencer. She could just imagine the look on his face were she to whisper it lovingly into *his* ear!

Elle unconsciously cleared her throat at the thought and turned back to the kitchen. She had to stay calm and keep herself from thinking the worst, unless the facts of the matter called for it. Right now, she was in the dark about those facts. For now, she might as well enjoy her time with Summer and get to know her (hopefully) future husband a little, in case …

… *in case what?* she thought as Spencer pulled a chair out for her at the dining room table. In case she was to marry him, or in case she couldn't? Which was it going to be? Until she heard from Mrs. Ridgley she had no idea. However, getting to know Spencer Riley "a little" would serve either way. If they did marry, she had a head start on getting to know him; if he arrested her and threw her in jail, maybe she would have softened him up a bit.

Logical. Yes, that's what it was – logical.

And logical is how she would remain until she heard from Mrs. Ridgley. That was her plan.

But sometimes, the best plans go awry.

"Well, what do you think?" Clayton asked as they fed their horses after supper.

Spencer tossed hay into his horse's stall. "She was pretty quiet tonight. Paid more attention to Summer than to me."

"That makes sense. She knows Summer – they grew up together in the orphanage. It's only natural that she'd be excited to see her and get reacquainted."

"She didn't come all the way out here to marry Summer. She came out here to marry me."

"You worry too much, little brother."

"That's because I have something to worry about. I envisioned all sorts of things I might find wrong with her that would give me an excuse to send her back, especially since I'm not the one that sent for her in the first place. I didn't count on the possibility … okay, it occurred to me, but I didn't *count* on the possibility that I might be a disappointment to *her*."

"What?" Clayton exclaimed as he plunged the pitchfork he was using into a pile of hay. "Spence, what are you saying?"

Spencer sighed. "I don't think she's too impressed with me."

"That is the most ridiculous thing I've ever heard! Of course she's impressed with you. Why else would she have traveled all this way?"

"Because she had to?"

"Spencer … you're imagining things. Give her some time. I'm sure that as soon as Miss Barstow and Summer have had a chance to reconnect, she'll have her eye on you."

"I don't know about that. She seemed more interested in our new deputy than in me at supper. In fact, she hardly said two words to me, but listened to everything *he* had to say…"

"*Everyone* was listening to what he had to say. Any story out of Clear Creek is … well … different. But that's beside the point. I'm sure you're more interesting to Miss Barstow than stories of Dukes and Princesses and whatever else goes on in Uncle Harlan's town."

Spencer tossed his pitchfork into the hay pile next to Clayton's. "I guess you're right. I can't expect her to fawn all over me the first day." He turned to his brother. "I'll give her until tomorrow to do it."

Clayton laughed, slapped him on the back, and putting his arm around him, walked his brother out of the barn and back to the house. He knew how many nudges he'd needed to woo his fair maid of the mail. Perhaps all Spence needed was a little shove.

The next day, Summer showed Elle around

the grounds – to be exact, the house and the barnyard. Elle helped her feed the chickens, water the cows (actually, break the ice in their troughs) and perform various other daily duties that needed to be tended to. The heavier work, Clayton would see to, and Spencer would also help when he had time.

"Do you like it here?" Elle asked.

"I love it!" Summer said. "The fresh air, the fields and orchards. I can't wait to see what it looks like in the spring when the apple blossoms come out."

"I'm sure it will be quite beautiful," Elle said as she twisted a piece of hay in her fingers.

"What's the matter? I know that look."

Elle looked at her friend. "I … nothing's the matter. I'm feeling overwhelmed, I guess. It's a lot to take in."

Summer knew it was more than that. "You do like Spencer, don't you?"

Elle tried to remain neutral, but she did have feelings. How could she not? Every time she looked at Spencer Riley her heart did a flip. Did the man have to be so handsome? Last night at supper, she did her best to avoid becoming too entranced with him, focusing all her attention on Mr. Turner instead. His tall tales were intriguing – she didn't believe half of what he'd said about his hometown of Clear Creek, but at least they kept her from staring moon-eyed at Spencer Riley for half the night!

"You'll like Spencer once you get to know him," Summer said, pulling from her thoughts.

"Oh, I'm sure I will."

"Elle, please tell me what is wrong. You're not the same."

Elle turned from Summer so she couldn't see the heat of shame creep into her cheeks. She needed to get to town and send that message! "You haven't seen me in awhile. Of course I'm not the same."

"It's only been a few months. You can't have changed that much in so little a time."

Elle faced her again. "I keep thinking about the others, the ones left behind at the orphanage. Among other things …"

"I think about them too, but there's nothing to be done about it now. No one has a birthday coming up, do they?"

"Yes, Sequoia. Sequoia Rose, remember her?"

"Isn't she the one that came from the orphanage that burned down?"

"Yes, the girl who never talks to anyone."

"She's a strange one … but she's a hard worker, and Mrs. Teeters adores her. I'm sure she and Mrs. Ridgley will be able to find her a husband somewhere."

Elle nodded sagely. All they could do for their fellow orphans was hope and pray that they were as blessed as Summer had been. Elle couldn't say she was blessed, not yet. "I really ought to get word to Mrs. Ridgley that I've arrived safely. I'm sure she'll want to know."

"You're right. We'll tell the men tonight when they come home. I'm sure Clayton wouldn't mind taking us to town tomorrow. I need a few things from Quinn's Mercantile, and

Mrs. Quinn should have some new fabrics in. We need to hurry and make your wedding dress!"

Elle audibly gulped. "Oh, yes. That."

"Elle, try not to sound so excited," Summer said sarcastically. "Tell me truly. Is Spencer not to your liking?"

"He answered Mrs. Ridgley's advertisement and I accepted his proposal. I can't very well back out."

"You could if you really wanted to. But I can't understand why you would."

Elle again turned away from her friend. "Perhaps he isn't so interested in me …"

"Of course he is!"

Which, she admitted to herself, she knew. But maybe if she managed to avoid him until she knew the situation in New Orleans, she wouldn't risk losing *her* heart to *him*. That was definitely a risk. She'd caught little glimpses of him the night before at supper – his smile, the way a dimple formed on his left cheek every time he laughed at something Mr. Turner said, his dark eyes, his thick dark hair. His voice was heavenly, and several times she wanted to imagine what it would be like to have him whisper to her as Clayton did with Summer. She wanted to work on her wedding dress, talk about flowers and wedding cake and punch and who was the local preacher, who would be coming, all the wonderful things one does when putting a wedding together.

But she couldn't. She had to find out what had happened first.

Elle swallowed hard, squared her shoulders and turned around to face Summer. "Well then, if you say he's interested, then I'll take your word for it."

Summer smiled. "At least he didn't shoot you in the foot the minute you got off the stage."

Both girls laughed at that. Summer had told her the entire story while Clayton and Spencer were in the barn doing some evening chores. It was hilarious, and not a little miraculous. Who would have thought such an accident could bring two people together?

But then, it wasn't shooting that Elle was worried about. Hanging, more like …

"Let's go inside and bake some cookies," Summer said as she turned and began to limp back toward the house. "Besides, we might end up with visitors later."

"Visitors?"

"Nowhere is a small town, and small towns like their gossip. By now everyone knows you're here, and someone's bound to drop by and say hello. Most likely, Nellie Davis," she added darkly.

"Who is Nellie Davis?"

"Trust me, you'll find out soon enough." Summer didn't wait for Elle to respond, but kept heading toward the house.

Whoever Nellie Davis was, she at least would offer Elle some distraction that afternoon. If she wasn't going to be able to get to town until the next day, she didn't want to keep thinking about her dilemma. Maybe she could just enjoy her day with Summer, and then stare at the handsome Spencer Riley when he got home later. She would at least allow herself that one small luxury.

What Elle didn't know, however, was that thanks to some prompting from Clayton, Spencer had more than staring at his future bride over the supper table in mind.

FIVE

As it turned out, Nellie Davis didn't show up that day at the Riley farm to inspect Spencer's new bride – nor the next day, nor the next. But that's not what had Elle chewing her nails (a bad habit of hers when she was nervous) and Mrs. Riley in a dither. It was the fact that neither Clayton nor Spencer had made time to take the women to town so they could start getting what they needed for the wedding. And in Elle's case, to wire Mrs. Ridgley and find out what chaos, if any, she'd left behind her.

The only good news was that Summer's limp was fast disappearing. Of course, Elle was happy for her friend, especially after hearing how hard it had been to get around on crutches for weeks on end, and barely get around at all before that. But despite the good news, Elle's mind was still on her own problem. She *had* to find out what happened to Jethro and the man she'd shot back in New Orleans. The only way to do that was to ask Mrs. Ridgley. But the only way to do *that* was …

"Elle! Didn't you hear me?"

She almost jumped out of her chair at the suddenness of the question. She looked up at Summer, who was sitting in a chair opposite hers in the parlor. They were doing the mending together. "I'm sorry, I was woolgathering a bit."

"A bit? I'd say more like a wheelbarrow full! What has you so out of sorts today?"

Elle set aside the shirt she'd been mending in her lap. It was one of Spencer's, and that didn't help her focus either. He'd been most attentive the last two nights after he got home, and was becoming harder for her to resist. "I was hoping to get into town today."

"Me too!" Mrs. Riley exclaimed as she came into the parlor. "And thank heaven, Clayton has finally agreed to take us! I would've said let's go ourselves, but with Summer not quite ready I didn't want to risk it! If something was to happen and we had to walk to town or back home, your poor foot might give out!"

Summer visibly cringed. "The thought of having to use crutches again doesn't hold much appeal," she agreed.

Clayton stepped into the parlor. "Ladies, if we're going to town, then let's hurry. I've got work to do later this afternoon around here, and Mr. Johnson needs some help over at his place. If you want to have a decent amount of time to shop, we need to go now."

"Isn't his grandson coming home soon?" Mrs. Riley asked. "You'd think he'd want to take over the farm for his grandfather."

"He'll be done with his schooling this spring," Clayton told her. "I hear Matthew

Quinn is coming home early, though. He's so far ahead of his class, he plumb graduated already. Mrs. Quinn says he'll be here in a couple of weeks."

The corners of Mrs. Riley's mouth curved up into a tiny smile. "Yes, dear. I already know." She turned on her heel and left the parlor to get her coat.

Clayton frowned as he watched her go, pushed his hat off his forehead, then put his hands on his hips.

"What's wrong?" asked Summer.

"She's up to something," he said in a low voice. "I know that look."

Elle turned to the front hall. She couldn't see her future mother-in-law, but could hear her humming a merry tune. "Up to something?"

"Oh, yes – trust me," Clayton began. "You'll soon learn, Miss Barstow, that your future mother-in-law is not all she appears. When she wants, she can be as canny and conniving as a Philadelphia ward politician. She's got something cooking and it's not in the kitchen!"

"Clayton," Summer began, her voice just above a whisper. "How do you know? She's been here with us since Elle arrived, no one has come or gone from the farm except you and Spencer. How can you think your mother's …?"

"Because I know my mother," he quickly insisted. "Now let's go."

Elle and Summer glanced at each other and shrugged. They obviously weren't going to find out what it was Mrs. Riley had "cooking" any time soon. So they put on their coats, bonnets and gloves, and together the four of them left for town.

Elle was excited to finally be going. What a relief to be able to send word to Mrs. Ridgley, and be one step closer to finding out what had happened! In the meantime, she'd only have to keep Spencer at a distance for a week or more at the most. A good thing, as that task was becoming harder by the minute, and who knows what today would bring while they were in town. Last night he'd hardly taken his eyes from her, and it made her entire body break out in gooseflesh. If he kept looking at her like that, she might crack under the pressure and not be able to look away. Then after supper, he'd offered to help her with the dishes, and standing in the kitchen next to him was pure heaven.

But she didn't dare allow herself the giddy sensation that being so close to him caused, nor how the feel of his arm against her shoulder warmed her entire being. How could this be happening? She didn't even know the man yet, and was doing her very best to *keep* from falling for him! Not until she heard from Mrs. Ridgley ... and maybe not even then, depending on the news.

The drive to town was chilly, and Elle and Summer huddled together in the back of the wagon. They sat atop some folded blankets, with the added warmth of a quilt to cover them, but the cold bit through it all and left Elle shivering. Still, she welcomed the cold – at least it distracted her from thoughts of Spencer!

"You're not used to this kind of weather

yet," Summer said, stating the obvious.

"I'm sure … t-t-t-to get used … used to it ev-v-ventually," Elle replied with chattering teeth.

Summer leaned over to whisper in Elle's ear. "Once you're married, you won't ever be cold at night anymore!"

Elle's eyes widened. "Summer James … I mean *Riley* … don't say such things!" Aside from issues of propriety, the thought of lying in Spencer's arms on a cold winter's night was too much to bear at present. Besides, what if Clayton and Mrs. Riley had heard her?

Summer giggled at the scold and adjusted the quilt around them.

It wasn't long before they got into town and pulled up in front of Quinn's Mercantile. Clayton set the brake and hopped down, then helped the women out of the wagon. Elle's feet were freezing, and it hurt when they touched the ground. She stomped them to get some feel back in them.

"Don't worry, you'll adjust to the cold in time," Clayton said. "I'm going over to the sheriff's office to see what Spencer's up to. You ladies take your time. Oh, and Ma?"

"Yes, dear?" Mrs. Riley asked as she headed for the steps to the mercantile.

He smiled and looked right at Elle. "Spencer said to spare no expense."

"Oh!" Mrs. Riley exclaimed as she spun to him. "Well, now this may turn out to be quite the adventure!"

Clayton's jaw tightened as he smiled. "Try to contain your excitement, Ma. We don't need you scaring people."

"I'm not scared," Summer quickly replied.

"Nor I," added Elle, sensing the other two women's delight.

"But I am," Clayton muttered as he turned on his boot heel and headed down the street to the sheriff's office.

Mrs. Riley and Summer laughed at his retreat. Both knew that Clayton watched over the farm's finances like a mother bear guarding her cubs. Spencer simply tossed his earnings into the pot, so to speak. For Spencer to say "spare no expense" meant just that – but for Clayton, there were usually some limits. Both brothers were incredibly generous with those they loved; Clayton was simply more practical.

But Mrs. Riley and Summer both knew Clayton wanted Spencer and Elle's wedding to be special, and was giving his blessing (as best he could) where the spending was concerned.

"Why, hello there!" A tall, thin, gray-haired woman called to the three women from behind the counter as they entered.

"Good morning, Mrs. Quinn!" Mrs. Riley called back as she wiped her feet on a small rug by the door. "We have lots of shopping to do this morning!"

Mrs. Quinn's face lit up at what she obviously deemed a call to battle. Her mouth formed into a bright grin as she clasped her hands together in front of her. "Wonderful! Where do we start?"

Mrs. Riley went straight to the store counter. "Let's start at the top and work our way down!"

"Brilliant!" Mrs. Quinn agreed and hurried around the counter to where Elle stood. "Now, off with your coat and bonnet so we can get started."

"My coat and bonnet? Why do I need to take them off?"

"Now don't ask questions, dear! We're experts at this sort of thing!" Mrs. Riley said.

"Experts?" Summer laughed. "I don't recall this much excitement when I went shopping for my wedding things."

"That was on account of your injury, dear. We didn't want to tire you out!"

"She's right, you know," Mrs. Quinn added. "We went easy on you."

Elle and Summer glanced at each other, concern on their faces. The two older women looked like a couple of contestants about to start a race.

"Now do as Mrs. Quinn says, dear – take off your coat and bonnet. And your gloves, while you're at it!"

Elle stood and stared at Mrs. Riley for a brief moment before she complied. How could she let Spencer spend money on her? What if they couldn't marry? How was she going to get out of this? She didn't want Mrs. Riley to go through all this trouble if … "If I decide I don't care for something we've purchased, can it be returned?"

Mrs. Quinn and Mrs. Riley went stock still as if she'd asked the most ludicrous question in the world. "Why, yes," Mrs. Quinn began hesitantly. "If you really think it's necessary.

You can exchange it or I can return your money ..."

"Oh, but come now, Miss Barstow ... no, Elnora!" Mrs. Riley said. "I've made up my mind to start calling you that from now on! We're here to buy your wedding things. Why in heaven's name would you ever need to return any of it?"

Elle swallowed and offered a weak smile. "What if ... something doesn't match?"

"Well, that's why we're all here to help you, dear – so we get it right the first time!"

"Yes... of course. But I do need to get to the telegraph office. Maybe I should take care of that first?"

Mrs. Riley and Mrs. Quinn came at her at once. "No time for cold feet now!" Mrs. Quinn said as she pulled Elle's coat off.

"You can do it when we're done!" Mrs. Riley added while she whisked away her bonnet. "Now, let's take a good look at your hair ... what color ribbons, do you think?"

"I have just the thing!" Mrs. Quinn said excitedly as she turned and hurried to a shelf behind the counter.

Elle sighed in resignation and looked to Summer, who stood to one side and did her best not to laugh. "Was it like this for you?"

"No, they were much calmer when I was here to get my wedding things."

"Wonderful," Elle mumbled under her breath. Wonderful for everyone but her, that is. She wanted to be able to enjoy the moment, but her only thought was to get to the telegraph office.

"But then, the Davises were present on that occasion … that put a damper on things."

"As they usually do," Mrs. Quinn added over her shoulder.

The door opened to pull Elle out of her silent lament. She turned and sucked in a breath at the handsome man that came into the mercantile. *Spencer!* She couldn't deny her attraction now – he was gorgeous!

He sauntered into the mercantile like he owned the place. "Hello, ladies," he drawled. "Having fun yet?"

"We're just getting started!" his mother said. "What are you doing here?"

"Can't I come say hello to my lovely bride?" he asked, going straight to Elle. "Hello sweetheart," he said in a low voice and tipped his hat.

Elle's entire body grew warm. *Sweetheart?* He hadn't used such an endearment when addressing her before. This was a first, and she hoped not the last – her face was tingling with delight. "Hello," she said shyly.

He stepped closer and looked into her eyes. "Find anything you like?"

Elle's breathing stopped. *Ohhhh, but she shouldn't be enjoying this so much!*

"Spencer, I told you we're just getting started!" his mother scolded. "Now if you don't mind, why don't you come back in an hour and check on things then?"

Spencer continued to look deeply into Elle's eyes. "Hmmm …," he mused, his voice rumbling in his chest as he drew closer. "Blue, I should think."

Elle tried to swallow, but all she could manage was a tiny gasp.

Spencer reached out and wrapped a tendril of her blonde hair around one of his fingers. "Blue would go so well with your eyes," he whispered as his own eyes roamed her face.

Oh God ... Elle felt her knees grow weak. He was so close she could smell the masculine scent of him. Not soap, not leather, not the wind and chill of the air outside. But *him*. She licked her lips in response.

He smiled as his eyes darkened. He leaned toward her even further.

"Spencer!"

Spencer and Elle jumped apart at his mother's voice.

"Get out of this store and come back in an hour!"

Spencer's jaw tightened but his smile remained. He tipped his hat once more to Elle before he turned and left the mercantile.

"Ah, young love ... the sight warms this old heart like nothing else," Mrs. Quinn said dreamily. "I can't wait until my Matthew comes home and ..."

"Land sakes!" Mrs. Riley interrupted. "Let's stop wasting time and get to work! Spencer will be back in an hour!" Elle caught the warning tone in her voice, and pondered what it was about.

Mrs. Quinn was coming around to the front of the counter, several boxes in hand, when the door once again opened.

"Oh, it figures…" Mrs. Riley said under her breath.

Elle looked at the door, then at Summer. "What is it?"

"Trouble, possibly," Summer muttered under her breath.

Abbey and Charlotte Davis came in and brushed snow from their coats near the door. Abbey looked up and took in the women. "Summer! I'm so glad to see you! Hello, Mrs. Riley, Mrs. Quinn!"

"Good morning, girls," Mrs. Quinn said happily. "Here to see the new fabrics I have in?"

"Yes, we are!" Abbey said as she happily walked over to a table laden with bolts of cloth.

"I have more in the back. I haven't had time to bring it all out – I've been busy getting Matthew's room ready. He comes home soon, you know."

"He does?" Abbey asked. "I thought colleges let out in the spring."

"He's home early on account of he's finished all his studies!" Mrs. Quinn said with pride. "He's the smartest boy in his class!"

"Life's going to seem incredibly dull here for him compared to Boston," Charlotte added dryly. "Why on earth would he want to leave an exciting city and come back to Nowhere?"

"Because he has kin here, girl. Why else?" Mrs. Quinn said sharply as she opened a box.

Mrs. Riley turned to Charlotte. "How's your mother, dear?" she asked, faking a smile.

"She's home sick with a cold. She sent us to

get her a few things."

"Oh, isn't that nice," Mrs. Riley replied. "I mean, that you've come to get her something."

Summer and Abbey both giggled at her slip. Charlotte didn't, but neither did she appear to notice it. She was too intent on the bolts of cloth in front of her.

Summer cleared her throat to get everyone's attention. "Ladies, may I present my friend Miss Elnora Barstow, Spencer's intended. Elle, this is Abbey Davis and her sister Charlotte. "

Elle took in the two girls. Summer had told her that Abbey was a real peach, but Charlotte could be as horrific as her mother. She'd shared some of her own experiences with the Davis family, and though she could laugh at them now, they certainly weren't funny at the time. Not only had Charlotte and her mother treated Summer like "poor white trash" at first, but they'd deceived her into leaving town instead of marrying Clayton, and Clayton into thinking she'd left because of him. All so Charlotte would have another shot at Clayton, who had absolutely no interest in marrying that tricksome Southern-belle wannabe. It was only Clayton's quick actions that saved her not only from the Davises' schemes, but from spoliation and death at an outlaw's hands. Summer was working on forgiving them, but forgetting was likely to be impossible.

Elle smiled and nodded to Abbey, who grabbed one of her hands and shook it enthusiastically. Charlotte, on the other hand, didn't so much as look at her.

"Charlotte, say hello to Miss Barstow," Abbey told her as she also caught her sister's aloof attitude.

Charlotte glanced to Elle, sighed, gave her a simple nod in greeting, then stiffly returned her attention to the fabric.

Abby rolled her eyes. "Never mind her. She's been like this the last week." Abbey leaned toward Summer and whispered. "It's been wonderful, really! She hasn't been this quiet since two years ago, when Clayton dumped water on her the first time she faked a swoon in front of him!"

Summer stifled a giggle, then looked to Elle. "Definitely the blue, like Spencer said."

Elle stared at the beautiful blue ribbons Mrs. Quinn held out before her. "They're lovely."

"They're yours," Mrs. Quinn happily said and returned them to their box. She set the box aside, then quickly followed Mrs. Riley to examine the bolts of cloth Charlotte was looking over.

"Are they going to pick out everything?" Elle asked Summer, astonished.

"No, you'll choose what you want. I think they just like the process more than anything else. They certainly did with me."

Elle smiled but thoughts of the telegraph office kept intruding. She needed to get her message sent!

"What's the matter?" Summer asked.

"Nothing," Elle said quickly.

"You don't look like you're having a very good time."

"Oh, I am!"

Summer took her by the elbow and steered her over to a display of shoes while Abbey joined the others. "Elle, are you *sure* you want to marry Spencer?"

Elle swallowed hard. This could be her one chance to gain more time. Even if she got her message out today, how long would it take for Mrs. Ridgley to get back to her? "I ... no, I'm *not* sure!"

Summer faced her. "I know that being a mail-order bride isn't like getting married the normal way. There's not much courtship, no months of getting to know one another. It's two people agreeing to make a life together so they can survive. But like the Good Book says, things are better with two. When one falls down, the other can lift them up. Two can stay warm better than one ..."

"I know that, but I'm just ... overwhelmed." Considering she didn't know if she'd be arrested by her future husband or not, it was an understatement.

"Yes, but you can't just put him off. You signed an agreement. Clayton and I had a few weeks to get to know each other because of my injury. Whether you wait another week, a month, or however long, it doesn't matter. Elle, you signed a contract." She shrugged and added, "Personally I don't know why you have cold feet. I can see you're attracted to Spencer."

Elle looked over her shoulder at the others, who were all admiring a bolt of cloth Spencer's mother was holding up. "I know I signed a contract. I just need a little more time. I … I really need to … to let Mrs. Ridgley know I got out here all right."

"You aren't going to wire her to tell her you want to go back, are you?"

"No! Of course not!" Going back was the *last* thing she wanted to do.

Summer's shoulders slumped as she relaxed. "I'm glad to hear it. I know you've been worried about getting to the telegraph office." She took Elle's hands in her own. "Please promise me you'll give Spencer a chance. He's a good man, and the Rileys are a wonderful family. Don't be hasty and make a wrong decision."

Elle felt a chill go up her spine. If only she could tell her friend what had happened … but she didn't dare. What would she do? They'd been taught at the orphanage to always do right by others and protect those they loved. But in this case, whom would Summer protect? Elle didn't want to put her friend in that sort of position, so it was better she remained quiet.

"I promise I'll give him a chance," Elle said, her heart in her throat. She hoped and prayed that Spencer Riley would do the same for her if it came down to having to tell him what she'd done.

SIX

Spencer walked slowly. Should he ignore his mother's request and go back to the mercantile? No, she said they'd be done in an hour, and if he showed up before then he'd get yelled at again. He could wait an hour, couldn't he? Oh, for heaven's sake, he was acting ridiculous! He was a grown man, not some idiotic schoolboy with his first crush!

But that's what he began to feel like when in Miss Barstow's company – and it was only getting worse. She was beautiful. She had spirit. She was a little odd at times, spontaneous, but he liked that – he didn't know what to expect from her and it kept him on his toes. Given a little more time he could easily fall in love with her.

She wasn't anything like he expected his mail-order bride to be. After finding out she'd come from the same orphanage as Summer, he'd figured she'd be calmer, more reserved like Summer … more in need of a hero, maybe. But Elnora Barstow would probably get along just as well without any man's help. He liked her independence, liked knowing that she might have needed his help to get out of New Orleans, but once free from there she wouldn't be leaning on him to make every decision, take charge of every situation. Shoot, with her gumption she could reject him, find herself a job, learn to use a gun, and be fine on her own!

The thought did send a shiver of worry through Spencer's veins. What if she didn't fancy him? She had acted rather ambivalent so far. She was polite, cordial, even laughed at his jokes, but he sensed she was holding back considerably. There was a stiffness about her, as if she sensed she might not be staying. At moments, in the set of her jaw or the look in her eye, it was as if she was battling with herself over him. Then it would be gone and she would relax and be light-hearted. She sure was a challenge to understand.

Thankfully, he liked challenges. He just hoped he was up to this one.

Spencer decided not to think on it further for the time being. He sighed and entered the sheriff's office – *his* office.

"Howdy, boss!" Billy Blake said. "Beautiful day, ain't it?"

Spencer looked at Billy, his other deputy. He was seated behind the desk with his feet propped up on it. "You're certainly happy this morning."

Billy removed his feet from the desk and sat up straight. "Got good reason to be. I'm courtin' Miss Abbey Davis! It's official – asked her pa and everythin'!"

Spencer smiled. Billy had been sweet on Abbey since November, and it appeared to be mutual. "Well, that's wonderful news! How's Mrs. Davis taking it?" Everyone knew that Nellie Davis, always the social climber, wanted her daughters married off to the wealthier families in the area. Her plan to wed Charlotte to Clayton had been thwarted by Summer's arrival – not to mention Charlotte's personality – and ever since Clayton and Summer's wedding at Christmas, Mrs. Davis had plunged herself into a new campaign to marry Abbey off to Spencer.

Mercifully, that plan had been stopped before it even got started. Abbey had only had eyes for Billy, and was smart enough to enlist her father's support in heading off her mother's scheme. Since the Christmas Eve debacle with Summer, Mr. Davis had been keeping a tighter rein on his headstrong wife – not surprising, after that mess had led to him pulling a gun on a sheriff (Clayton, at the time).

"Not too well. She's been kinda stand-offish, last few times I went over to see Abbey. But Mr. Davis invited me to Sunday supper this week!"

"That ought to drive Mrs. Davis plumb loco!" Spencer laughed. Billy grew up poor in Alabama, and his closest brush with being a gentleman was making sergeant in the Confederate Army during the war – three weeks before Lee surrendered.

"She kept askin' 'bout you the other day, though."

Spencer cringed. That could only mean that

Nellie still had her eye on him for Charlotte, and her husband hadn't blocked it yet. Considering Charlotte's behavior the day Miss Barstow came to town, she was probably counting on her mother to see it done, figuring if she couldn't have Clayton, she'd settle for the next closest.

He suspected it wasn't the Riley men so much as the Riley land Mrs. Davis wanted to welcome into her family. They had one of the larger orchards in the area, large enough to have leased part of it out to Mr. Johnson, their neighbor, when Clayton and Spencer had decided to try their hands as lawmen. But Old Man Johnson was slowing down, Clayton was leaving the sheriff's duties behind to spend more time with Summer, and so they'd agreed to end the lease come spring. Clayton and Spencer had also decided that if it got too much for Clayton and a couple of hands to handle, Spencer would turn his badge over to someone else and return to apple farming himself.

"What exactly did she ask?" Spencer finally said as he hung up his hat and coat.

"Well, she didn't ask so much 'bout you as she did 'bout yer weddin'."

"She knows we haven't had a wedding yet, doesn't she?"

"Oh, trust me, she knows! She was makin' all kinds of comments to Charlotte while me and Abbey was sittin' in the parlor. They was in the dinin' room, but we could hear ev'ry word."

Spencer rolled his eyes. "I can only imagine what they were saying, but tell me anyway."

"Well, it amounted to if'n you wasn't hitched

yet, it must mean you don't care for yer mail-order bride, and there weren't no good reason why you hadn't got hitched New Year's Day when she got off the stage."

Spencer turned to him. "You know, my mother wanted just that, but I thought it'd be better to give Miss Barstow and I a couple of weeks to get acquainted. I saw how it helped Clayton and Summer, not to mention how important it is to be able to trust the other person and how to start to grow that trust. Remember that while you're courting Abbey."

Billy nodded. "Yeah, that's important to womenfolk – the whole trust thing."

"To men too. Trust is what binds two people together. You have to have it. I want to start building some of that with Miss Barstow before we marry."

"What about them folks that marry the same day the bride gets off the stage?"

"It might work for some people, but I'd rather have time for courting, even if we are already contracted to marry."

Billy sagely nodded in agreement. "Works for me, boss."

"So how's our new deputy?" Spencer asked to change the subject. He was having a hard enough time trying to woo his future bride, and didn't want to talk about it anymore.

"Aw, he's fittin' right in. He went along with Doc Brown to the Miller place. I didn't think ya'd mind so I let him go. Doc can't get enough o' Tom's stories 'bout the doc down in Clear Creek. The way he tells it, Doc Drake is some kind o' miracle worker."

Spencer smiled and sat on the desk. "Mr. Turner sure does love his hometown. I wonder how long he'll stay in Nowhere? I should wire Uncle Harlan and ask if we can keep him for a while."

"Better to just ask Tom Turner if'n he wants to stay on permanent."

"You're right. In fact, I'll do both." In fact, he should put his hat and coat back on and go wire Uncle Harlan right now – then he could just *happen* to go by the mercantile again. And didn't Miss Barstow want to wire that mail-order bride agency she came from? That was a fine coincidence, wasn't it?

Unfortunately, Spencer never got the chance.

Abbey came through the door to the sheriff's office, saw Billy, and went straight for him, leaving her sister behind on the boardwalk. "Hello, Billy," she said shyly.

Billy stood, puffed his chest out and moseyed from behind the desk. He brushed his reddish hair out of his eyes and smiled. "Howdy, Miss Abbey. What brings you here?"

"Daddy wanted me to tell you to bring a healthy appetite come Sunday. I'm making a pot roast and apple pie."

Charlotte stood in the doorway, her face sour as a barrel of vinegar, and rolled her eyes.

"Pot roast is my favorite! I can't wait."

Abbey gazed at him with a look that clearly said *I'm yours forever!*

Spencer began to wonder if he'd ever see that same look on Miss Barstow's face when he felt Charlotte tap him on the shoulder. He turned, reluctantly, and looked at her. She had a forlorn look he'd never seen before, and his face changed to one of concern. "Are you okay, Charlotte?"

"Oh … I'm fine," she sighed theatrically. "I'm just busy preparing myself for the inevitable."

Dear Lord have mercy, he thought. He should've known better than to think this was anything but another one of her put-ons. Forget Nowhere, Washington – Charlotte belonged in Philadelphia, on stage at the Chestnut Street Theater in a production of some awful melodrama. "Inevitable what?"

Her mouth sagged into a pout. "Spinsterhood."

Spencer struggled not to roll his eyes. While it would be a benefit for the male population at large, spinsterhood and the man-hungry Charlotte Davis would go together about as well as fried chicken and turpentine. She was going to land herself a man no matter what, and not only did everyone in town know it, most of them were already feeling sorry for him, whoever he turned out to be. "I don't think you really have to worry about that," he replied neutrally, though he almost thought he saw a flicker of honest worry in her eyes.

"Oh, I can see it coming. Everyone in this

town will wind up with someone, everyone but me. Too bad they don't have mail-order grooms. I might as well order up one."

"Well, there's no such thing as far as I know. But someone will come along, Charlotte. You'll see." *The poor dolt.*

"Will I? Your brother is taken, and you'll end up married to … to that girl. Where does that leave me?" She cast her eyes downward.

Spencer fought the urge to laugh – she was definitely playing the sympathy card. And he did feel sorry for her, though not in the way she intended. She had a well-earned reputation for being haughty, sharp-tongued, stuck-up and a gossip, in addition to a man-chaser. It would be hard work to repair that sort of a reputation in order to find a husband in a small, close-knit town like Nowhere.

She didn't always used to be this bad. She'd gotten worse over the last few years, largely thanks to Mrs. Davis' expert tutelage. But unless Charlotte left the Davis household, how would she ever be able to change? The more Spencer thought on it, the more truth he suspected there was of her possibly becoming a spinster – more truth than she knew.

"Oh, Charlotte!" Abbey scolded. "Stop being so dramatic!"

"Easy for you to say – you have a beau." Charlotte shot back then turned her attention to Spencer. "You'll think of me, won't you, if that girl leaves and goes back to wherever it was that she came from?"

"What are you playing at, Miss Davis?"

Spencer replied, Charlotte's machinations with Summer still fresh in his mind.

She turned away and took a few steps toward the cell area located down the back hall. "Well, I'm not one to gossip …"

"Charlotte!" Abbey interjected. "You're *usually* the one to gossip!"

Charlotte shot her a warning look. "As I was going to say, your future bride did seem a bit distracted in the mercantile while we were there."

Spencer immediately turned to Abbey. "Is this true?"

Abbey shrugged. "Well, yes, she didn't seem very focused on picking out things for a wedding. But I doubt it had anything to do with you or going back or anything like that," she finished, glaring at her older sister as if daring her to press the point.

Spencer's heart sank – despite Abbey's assurances, maybe Miss Barstow wasn't all that interested in him. That didn't mean he was going to take the conniving Charlotte's word for it, however. "I'll bear that in mind. But Charlotte, if I find out you've tried to alienate her affections, I will arrest you." He rested his hand on the Colt in his holster, just to underscore the point.

The reactions he got were priceless. Billy's eyes looked about to fall out of his head. Abbey smiled like the entertainment was about to start. And Charlotte went white as a sheet. "Well … we'd best be going, Abbey. Mother will want her tea and we still have to stop by Mrs.

Jorgensen's." she said nervously. "It was nice stopping in for a visit … Sheriff."

Spencer gave her a half-hearted smirk. "You ladies have a nice day."

"Five o'clock, Billy – don't forget!" Abbey called over her shoulder as Charlotte dragged her toward the door.

"I'll be there with bells on – nothin' I like better'n a good pot roast! 'Cept maybe the pretty gal cookin' it."

Abbey blushed crimson and smiled as Charlotte hauled her out the door and slammed it shut. Spencer and Billy both cringed at the noise.

"I feel so sorry for the fella that winds up married to Charlotte," Billy said. "Would you *really* try an' arrest her?"

"There isn't any 'try' about it – I'm not sure about Washington Territory, but there are laws against turning one spouse away from another in a lot of states. Even if I couldn't make it stick, it would be a black mark on her. She'd have to start considering spinsterhood for real."

"Whoo-ee, Spencer, you are playin' with fire!"

"I saw how she and her mother tried to break up my brother and sister-in-law. I have had quite enough of her games." Spencer finally smiled. "But what about the fellow that marries into that family? You won't only have Nellie Davis as a mother-in-law, you'll have Charlotte for a sister-in-law!"

"Don't think I ain't thought about that! Which is why you'd best get down to the telegraph office and wire yer Uncle Harlan. 'Cause if me an' Abbey get married, we ain't staying here!"

"What?"

"Ya heard me. I talked to Clayton about it when Tom Turner got to town. I didn't wanna leave ya short-handed, but if he stays on and yer able to hire on another deputy, then Abbey an' I can go elsewhere. Plenty o' places lookin' for experienced lawmen."

Spencer gave him the eyebrow, "Have you talked with Abbey about this?"

"Sure have. She's on board, an' she thinks she can talk her pa into lettin' us. We ain't stayin' in Nowhere and puttin' up with Nellie and Charlotte – 'cept maybe on Christmas."

"Sounds like a plan, then. Keep a lid on things until I get back." Spencer grabbed his coat and hat, and left for the telegraph office. He might as well stop by the mercantile and take Miss Barstow with him, as it had been at least *close* to an hour and he knew she wanted to wire New Orleans. Maybe that's what had her so distracted – she might be the sort that had to have everything done that needed doing before she could relax and enjoy herself.

Well, if that was the case, he could help her with that, and she should be more open to some good old wooing and courting. He didn't fancy going into a marriage with a woman who didn't think highly of him, or with whom he didn't share a mutual attraction. He hoped that wasn't part of her problem. That would be a slap in the face, to find she didn't find him the least bit attractive! The thought pained him, and he picked up his pace.

When he reached the mercantile, he found Miss Barstow draped in several bolts of white and ivory cloth – he could see very little of her dress underneath. A painting he'd once seen of a Greek goddess flashed through his mind. She was beautiful, and it hurt him to think this lovely creature might have no interest in him.

"Spencer, what are you doing here?" It's only been … oh, I guess it has been an hour!" His mother seemed disappointed as she and Mrs. Quinn continued to wrap Miss Barstow up in bolts of cloth.

Miss Barstow sent him a pleading look, and he quickly took the cue. "I need to borrow my bride, Ma. I have to wire Uncle Harlan, and figured Miss Barstow could accompany me to the telegraph office. I know she wanted to wire New Orleans."

"Oh yes!" Miss Barstow exclaimed. "Yes, I do!"

Ah – that *was* what was holding her back. He smiled at the thought that Abbey had been right and Charlotte wrong, and strode over to the group. Summer, he noticed, was sitting in a chair by the pot-bellied stove and reading *Silas Marner*. She smiled at him and winked. Apparently he must've come just in time to keep his mother and Mrs. Quinn from driving the younger women crazy. "If you don't mind, Ma, we won't be gone long. Then you can finish up here."

His mother sighed in resignation. "Oh, very

well. But hurry right back! I suppose Mrs. Quinn and I can start cutting fabric for the dress while you're gone." She turned to Miss Barstow. "You said you liked the ivory lace best, dear?"

Miss Barstow did her best to extricate herself from her wrappings. "Yes, that will do nicely. Thank you, Mrs. Riley – and I promise I'll be right back!"

Spencer noted the excitement in her voice, smiled again and stepped over to help unwind his future bride – his mother and Mrs. Quinn had her wrapped up like Lazarus in his tomb. As soon as he was done, he held his arm out to her. "Shall we?"

She smiled up at him in relief, grateful to be free of her bindings and the older women's attentions. More important, she would finally be able to send that telegram! "Yes!"

He chuckled, then steered her toward the coat rack by the door. Yessiree, there was no stopping him now. He was going to woo the stockings off of his future wife. By the time they were married, she would be madly in love with him!

Spencer Riley might be a worrier, he thought to himself, but he did nothing halfway.

SEVEN

At last, Elle could finally get a message off to Mrs. Ridgley! Now all she had to do was wait for a reply – which shouldn't take more than a few days – and she could move on with her life. That is, with luck and a positive reply from Mrs. Ridgley. If it were bad news, however ...

"Did you find everything to your liking? For the wedding, I mean?"

Elle shook herself back to the present and looked up at the man she was (hopefully) to marry. "Yes, thank you for asking. Your mother certainly does love to put together weddings!"

"You have no idea. She and Mrs. Quinn have had their hands in more weddings in these parts than I can count. Now that she has her own sons marrying, she's beside herself. You should have seen her with Summer and Clayton's wedding."

"I thought she went easy on Summer."

"Summer, yes, but not Clayton. Ma about drove him crazy with her wedding talk, on and on, for weeks after Summer arrived. If it hadn't been for her injury, Ma would've gotten things underway a lot sooner and had them married off well before Christmas. As it turned out though, things worked out for the best and they were married just after midnight Christmas Day."

"How romantic! I didn't realize they were married around midnight – I thought it was sometime late Christmas morning."

"No. They had their wedding and their wedding night in a matter of hours."

Elle felt herself blush at his remark, knowing what he meant. She hadn't thought about that aspect of marriage since leaving New Orleans, but she'd pondered it before, and wondered what it would be like. Mrs. Teeters had given her a brief talk about marital relations, but no real details. She figured she was just going to have to wait to find out – until she discovered that Summer was now to be her sister in-law! When they had some privacy, she'd ask her all about it.

But right now, she had to send that message! "Thank you so much for bringing me with you to the telegraph office. I know Mrs. Ridgley must be wondering why she hasn't heard from me."

"I'm sorry for not taking you sooner, but I've been pre-occupied with other things," he said, giving her a pointed look.

Did he mean her? Well, what else could he mean? "I'm sorry if I've kept you from your work."

"What? Oh no, you mustn't worry about that. My wife comes first. It's just that … well, maybe since I knew you'd arrived safe and sound, I wasn't thinking about getting word to

Mrs. Ridgley. But how is she to know unless you tell her? I apologize for keeping you away this long – it was selfish of me."

"It's okay. The important thing is that I'm letting her know. I suppose a few days' delay doesn't hurt anything." *Except that they've been like torture!* She looked at him and smiled as they approached the telegraph office.

"Besides, I should have sent word to Uncle Harlan that Tom Turner arrived. I must be more preoccupied than I thought."

She smiled again as they entered the telegraph office, but said nothing. If he had been preoccupied with her this whole time, what must he think of her? She hadn't avoided him entirely – that would have been impossible – but she hadn't exactly fallen all over him either. He probably wondered if she was attracted to him at all. But she didn't feel safe returning his attentions until she knew what she was facing – wedded bliss? Or the gallows?

What *did* they do to women out West who were convicted of murder? Hanging? Firing squad? Something particularly "Western" like being abandoned in the desert or dragged behind a mustang? She couldn't bear to think of it! *Be logical, Elle! It was self-defense! The man was coming at you with a gun! He had already shot Jethro, and ...*

"What did you want to say?"

Elle jumped. "Oh!" She looked up at him, eyes wide.

His brow furrowed as he quickly studied her. "What's wrong?"

"N-nothing. Give me a few minutes – you go ahead and, and send yours first."

His eyes lingered on her a moment in concern, before he turned to a man sitting behind the counter and began to tell him what he wanted sent.

Elle swallowed hard and turned away from him as she wracked her brain over what to say, what would convey what she so desperately needed to know without giving it away to Spencer …

"Miss Barstow?"

Elle stiffened.

Spencer put his hands on her shoulders and turned her around to face him. "Elnora … may I call you Elnora? We *are* to be married soon, after all."

She looked into his eyes. He had a starry expression on his face that made her tingle all over. He was attracted to her, that was obvious. But how was she going to keep her own heart in check until she received a response from Louisiana? He was so handsome and strong and, most importantly, *hers!* She wished she could let her heart fly! But she didn't dare, not until she knew she bore no guilt in what had happened, not until she'd found out if Jethro was all right.

"You can call me Elle. Everyone did at the orphanage."

"Elle," he said as if trying it out. "I like it. You can send your message now."

She looked at the man sitting behind the counter and swallowed, then approached,

Spencer right behind her. "Hello," she said weakly.

"Well?" the man asked impatiently. "What's your message?"

"Oh, yes. My message." She smiled nervously. "To Mrs. Ridgley, Ridgley Mail-Order Bride Service, New Orleans. 'Arrived safely. Give Jethro my best regards and thanks. Please inform me of his welfare. E.B.'"

"That's it?" the man asked.

"Yes." She turned to Spencer. "That's not too long, is it?"

"No, it's fine." Spencer watched as the man scribbled the message down. "Who is Jethro?"

Elle briefly closed her eyes. She knew he might ask, but it couldn't be helped. She didn't know how else to word the message. "One of Mrs. Ridgley's … business associates. He was kind enough to see me to the train station. He … he wasn't feeling very well when I left."

"Oh, I'm glad to hear Mrs. Ridgley sees to every detail. If anyone else in town is looking for a mail-order bride, Clayton and I will definitely recommend her establishment."

She smiled at him. "I'm sure she'll be pleased. Um … how long do you think before I'll get a reply?"

"Reply? To what?"

"The message I'm sending?"

"Oh, that. Generally a lot of folks don't reply at all. It costs money. But I do recall that Clayton heard back from Mrs. Ridgley when he sent word that Summer got here. I think he left out the part about shooting her, though …"

Elle couldn't help but laugh, but she was still nervous. She just wanted this whole thing to be done with so she could get on with being the bride she was sent here to be. Easier said than done. Now all she could do was wait. "How long before he heard from her? Do you remember?"

"Hmm, let me see … maybe a week or two? To tell you the truth, I don't quite recall."

Elle's heart sank. How long would she have to wait, then? And what happened if she didn't hear back at all? What if the gunman had died, and she was charged with his murder? There were so many unanswered questions! Her stomach knotted, and she put a hand to her temple to still the throbbing ache that began every time she thought about the whole mess.

"Are you all right?" Spencer asked, concerned. He took her by the elbow and steered her to a corner of the telegraph office, then turned her to face him and looked her over. "I've noticed something is troubling you, ever since you arrived…"

Elle's eyes widened at his words. Oh, no! What was she going to tell him? Was *not* telling him what was wrong same as lying? She supposed that as long as there wasn't any asking going on, then no. But now he *was* asking … "I … I'm just overwhelmed with … what it took to get here, with finding Summer again …"

"But wasn't finding Summer a good thing?"

"Oh, yes, of course! But …"

"Is it me, Elle? Aren't you happy to be here?"

She looked into his eyes. Was he worried she didn't want to be there? If she put herself in his place, how would she react to her behavior since her arrival? She moaned at the thought and looked at the floor.

"Miss Barstow … Elle … you might as well know the truth."

Her head snapped up.

"I didn't send for you."

Her mouth dropped open like a heavy drawbridge. "Wh-what?"

He took a deep breath, glanced about and in a low voice said, "I didn't send away for you. My mother did."

She backed up a step. What was he saying, that he didn't want her? That it wasn't his idea to send away for a mail-order bride in the first place? "I don't understand."

He closed the distance between them. "I want nothing but honesty between us. I won't start our marriage out with anything that might mislead each other. So … I wasn't the one who answered the advertisement for a mail-order bride. My mother was."

She said nothing. All she could do was stand and stare. After all she'd gone through to get here – the risk, not knowing if Jethro lived or died, if she had killed a man to protect him – it was all too much. Her knees gave way, and down she went.

"Elle!" Spencer cried as he caught her before she hit the floor. He pulled her into his arms and held her close. "Elle?!"

She didn't answer. She couldn't answer.

What would she say?

She was suddenly aware her feet no longer touched the ground, and realized Spencer was carrying her across the telegraph office to a chair by a pot-bellied stove. He carefully set her down in it, then took one of her hands in his. "Elle, are you all right? Say something!"

She looked at him numbly. If he didn't send away for her, then what was she doing here? And why did he want to marry her if he hadn't wanted a mail-order bride in the first place? Was he doing this just to please his mother? What was going on?

"Elle, I'm sorry if I've upset you. Let's go back to the farm – I'll explain everything."

"Your mother … Summer …," she said weakly. "Waiting at the … mercantile ..." It was all she could manage at the moment as realization sank in. He really didn't want her – he was just marrying her to please his mother.

So where did that leave her? She wanted to have love in a marriage, not this. And even if Spencer really wasn't interested in her, she probably couldn't go back to New Orleans. Even if Jethro made a full recovery and the man she shot was also still alive, that would just leave her right back where she'd started ... only without the stage and train fare to make it back. No, that was no solution.

That left only one clear option. If Spencer Riley truly did not desire her, she could not in clear conscience marry him. Instead, she'd have to find a way to make it on her own in Nowhere.

"Elle, look at me." Spencer tucked a finger

under her chin and tilted her face up to his. "Don't misunderstand me. I'm not saying I don't like you."

"But you don't want me, either," she replied, as sharply as she could in her state. Why hadn't he brought this up days ago, when she'd first arrived?

"Let's get back to the others and then go home. It will be easier to explain everything with Clayton and Summer …"

"Sheriff!"

Elle and Spencer both looked up to find Tom Turner, the new deputy, standing in the doorway of the telegraph office, his face red from exertion. "What is it, Tom?" Spencer asked.

"You'd best come quick like. There's been an accident."

Spencer pulled Elle up from the chair, took her by the arm and began to usher her toward the door. "Has anyone gone to fetch Doc Brown?"

"Sir, it *is* Doc Brown!"

Spencer's eyes became round as saucers. "What? *Doc's* been in an accident?"

"Yessir. We rode out to the Miller place and saw to Mrs. Miller's younguns, then on the way back one o' the horses threw a shoe. When Doc and I got outta the wagon to check on the horse, the fool thing kicked him right in the head! I got him into the wagon and came straight back to town. His wife Milly is asking for ya!"

"Oh, my Lord. Did you take him to his place?"

"Yessir, but I had to ask where it was. I don't

know my way 'round yet. Some o' the menfolk helped me get him out o' the wagon, then Milly sent me to fetch ya. Yer ma said I'd find you here. You'd best hurry!"

Spencer gave him a curt nod. "Could you escort Miss Barstow back to the mercantile for me?" He turned to Elle. "I'm so sorry, sweetheart. I'll have Mr. Turner take you home. I'll join you later. See to it, will you, Tom?"

"Yessir, Sheriff."

Spencer hurried out the door, down the street and out of sight. Elle stood speechless next to the new deputy and stared after him. After a moment, she spoke. "How badly was the doctor hurt?"

"Looked pretty bad, ma'am. That fool horse knocked him clean out – he still hadn't come to when I left his house. I've seen what a horse can do to a man if'n one kicks hard enough."

"What is Sheriff Riley going to be able to do for him? He's not a doctor of any sort, is he?"

"No, ma'am, not that I know of. But the way Doc Brown done explained things, the Riley boys are like family to 'im. The doc's wife didn't ask me to fetch Sheriff Riley because he could do anything to help – she asked me to fetch 'im in case Doc Brown don't wake up."

Tears stung Elle's eyes at his words. Summer had mentioned a strong kinship between the Rileys and Browns, but she didn't understand how strong until now.

"I'd best take ya home now, ma'am."

She looked up into the deputy's blue eyes and saw deep concern in them. "Do you think

Doc Brown will be all right?"

"Can't say, ma'am. I'm no sawbones, but … well … I need to get ya home now. Let's go fetch your family from the mercantile and be on our way." He motioned toward the door with one hand. Doc Brown must be very bad off, she realized.

She followed Tom Turner back to the mercantile where Summer waited, but there was no sign of Ma Riley. "There you are!" Mrs. Quinn exclaimed as they came through the door.

"Where's Mrs. Riley?"

"She's gone to Doc and Milly's place. She told me to wait here for you," Summer said.

"I'm to take ya both on home," Tom told her.

"But then how will my mother-in-law get home? She can't very well ride home on the back of Spencer's horse. Thank you, sir, but we really should wait for her here. Clayton drove us here, so he can drive us home."

"I don't mind," Mrs. Quinn volunteered.

"Where is Clayton?" Elle asked.

"I don't know," Summer answered. "I think Billy went to look for him the moment he heard what happened." She turned to Tom. "Have you seen my husband?"

"No, ma'am."

Summer looked at Elle, her brow raised in question. "Where on earth could he be?"

EIGHT

"But Clayton, she's clearly not interested in your brother! Talk to Spencer and send her back before she breaks his heart."

Clayton eyed Charlotte. Even if he'd thought what she was saying was true – and from what he'd seen, it just might be – he still automatically thought she was up to no good. "I wouldn't count on Miss Barstow going anywhere."

She smiled prettily up at him. "Oh, but I just don't want to see Spencer get hurt."

Clayton's expression was blank. The next time Charlotte Davis worried about someone else getting hurt would likely be the first …

"Here's your mama's dress, Charlotte," Mrs. Jorgensen said, setting a wrapped package on the counter. Clayton had gone to the dressmaker's shop to order a new dress for Summer. The annual Valentine's dance was always a festive event in Nowhere, and he thought the gift of a new outfit from the only dressmaker in town would be a fine gift for the occasion. Unfortunately, he'd run into Charlotte picking up a dress Mrs. Jorgensen had mended for her mother. Even though Abbey was a fine seamstress, Nellie Davis insisted on having Mrs. Jorgensen do her mending.

Mrs. Jorgensen looked expectantly at Clayton. "What can I do for you?"

"I'm here about a dress for my *wife*." He emphasized the last word for Charlotte's benefit – it was the closest he, as a gentleman, could come to saying *I don't trust you* to her face.

Charlotte visibly cringed at the word, and turned her back on him. "I'll just be going now. But heed what I say, Clayton. It's for Spencer's own good."

"Of course it is, Charlotte." The sarcasm was clear.

Mrs. Jorgensen raised an eyebrow and quickly looked at Charlotte to gauge her reaction.

"It is! Believe it or not, Clayton Riley, my intentions are … honorable."

Clayton just managed not to laugh. Anything coming out of Charlotte's mouth was usually far from honorable. "I'll be sure to keep that in mind," he replied in the same skeptical tone.

She ignored his intent. "Thank you. I appreciate it. Now I'd best be getting on home. Abbey's probably halfway there by now."

"You're walking? Didn't you bring the buggy?" Clayton asked.

"Of course, but Abbey took it on home. I decided to walk."

Clayton immediately looked at her feet, and saw a fancy pair of heeled boots – not the sort of footwear for walking a mile or so across icy dirt roads. She probably planned this. But if she did, she was in for a big surprise. "You know you can't walk all the way home in those shoes. Your feet will be blistered and frozen by the time you get there. What were you thinking, letting Abbey go on home ahead of you?"

"I … just … felt like a walk."

"You felt like a flirt," Mrs. Jorgensen quipped as she turned from the counter to go into the back room of her shop.

Charlotte glared after her, then turned to Clayton. "I've had a lot of thinking to do lately, that's all. I think better when I walk," she added, straightening up proudly.

"Mrs. Jorgensen!" Clayton called, ignoring her response. "I'll be back tomorrow. Pink! I want pink! I'll look at your fabric then!" He grabbed Charlotte by the arm and pulled her toward the door.

"Clayton Riley, unhand me! You don't have the right to manhandle me just because my shoes–"

"Would you rather walk home, Charlotte? This is what you planned, isn't it – that I drive you home?"

She looked up at him, her face red. "I can walk just as easily! I don't have to let you drive me h–"

"Those shoes are not fit for this weather and you know it!"

"Well, I never–"

She didn't get to finish. Clayton opened the door, dragged her through, then pulled her along beside him toward the mercantile and his wagon. He glanced down, noted the smiled on Charlotte's face, and almost smiled himself as he led her past the wagon to the mercantile's steps.

"Where are you going?" she squeaked. "Aren't you taking me home?"

"Of course – but first I need to fetch my wife."

Charlotte's face fell. "Oh. I quite forgot about her."

"I'm sure you did," he said as he shoved her through the mercantile door.

"Clayton!" Summer cried. "Where have you been?" Her eyes landed on Charlotte. "And what have you been doing?" she added, her nose wrinkling in distaste.

Charlotte smiled prettily at her and wrapped her arm through Clayton's. "Clayton offered to take me home."

Summer looked at Clayton, one eyebrow up, waiting for an explanation.

"There's been an accident," Elle interjected. "It's Doc Brown. Spencer and your mother are already at the doctor's house."

Clayton shook Charlotte off his arm like she was a spider. "What? What happened?!"

"Doc Brown got kicked in the head by his horse coming back from the Miller's place," Summer told him. "Milly wants you over there right away."

"Good God! Stay here, then – I'll be back as soon as I can!" He turned and hurried from the mercantile.

Charlotte watched him go with a look of defeat. "I might as well walk home, then."

Summer had had enough. "Is that all you care about? Can't you think of anyone besides yourself? Doc Brown could be dying!"

Charlotte raised her chin. "What would you know of it? And who says I'm thinking of myself? But if I am, why in heaven's name would I want to stay here with the likes of you?"

Elle gasped at her rudeness. Summer, who'd seen Charlotte's act before, only rolled her eyes in scorn.

"Well, I'll just see myself home, thank you very much!" Charlotte spun on her heel and stomped toward the door.

Elle watched as she stormed out into the cold and down the stairs into the street. "How far out of town does she live?"

"Not far enough," Summer whispered to herself. Then, to Elle: "A little over a mile, if I remember right. I was only there once – and once was enough for me."

"It's terribly cold out to be walking that far …"

Summer closed her eyes a moment. "I know. And that's what she wants you to think. She was hoping to weasel a ride home with somebody." She shook her head. "That spoiled little rich girl irritates me to no end."

"I can see that, but …"

"You call her back if you want, Elle. But I won't. She's trouble with a capital T."

Elle thought about it a moment. She'd witnessed that sort of defiant behavior in the orphanage. It was easy to see Charlotte Davis was defiant, and to speculate on how she could have gotten that way. Even if it was her own doing, rejection was a cruel master. Any orphan knew that.

Elle took a deep breath and went to the door. Sure enough, there was Charlotte standing at the bottom of the mercantile's porch steps, her shoulders heaving from her tears. So she wasn't so feisty after all. But were her tears real?

Elle had a feeling she might regret this, but … "Miss Davis," she called out the door. "Won't you come back inside where it's warm? I'm sure either Clayton or Spencer will be back with Mrs. Riley, and we can take you home then."

Charlotte turned toward her. Her eyes were indeed red from crying. "Well, I suppose I could do that." She wiped at her tears. "And I could do with a licorice whip." She lifted her skirts as she ascended the stairs, and brushed past Elle when she opened the door for her. She watched as the girl went straight to the store counter. "Mrs. Quinn?" Charlotte called. "Some service, please!"

Elle sighed, closed the door, and went to join Summer – who was shaking her head and silently laughing to herself – near the stove.

"I can't lose him, Clayton! I just can't!" Milly Brown cried before burying her face in her hands.

"He'll pull through, Milly. I know he will," Clayton said to console her. But he didn't know, not at all.

"Milly, we've made him as comfortable as possible," Spencer added. "What else do you want us to do?"

"I … I don't want to be alone with him. What if he wakes up and wants out of bed? You know how stubborn he is!"

"One of us will stay, then," Spencer offered.

"I'll stay – you take the women home," Clayton told him.

Spencer nodded his agreement, then looked at their mother as she tucked a quilt around Doc Brown. "You've seen this sort of injury before, Milly," she said. "You know he can pull through. And we'll be praying."

"I know, Leona. But I also know that half the time, folks don't recover. He might never wake up ..." She began to weep again.

"Now don't you be thinking that!" Mrs. Riley scolded. "Doc's a stubborn man, just like you said – too stubborn to die on us! Isn't that right, Clayton?"

Clayton put an arm around his mother. "That's right. If anyone knows that, it's me. Now, Milly, how about some of your famous soup? If I have to stay here and be just as stubborn as Doc, I can't do it on an empty stomach."

Milly smiled through her tears. "I ain't arguing he's gonna die. I'm just being practical about it. Dying is just a part of living, that's all.

But I don't want to lose him …" she said as her tears fell freely once again.

"And you won't – not if we have any say in it," Spencer said. "You let Clayton take care of things tonight, and help you with Doc when he wakes up. He's gonna be mad as a rattler and want to shoot that horse of his – Clayton will have to talk him out of it."

"That's right," Clayton agreed. "That's a mighty fine horse Doc has – it would be a shame to shoot it over one kick."

"Oh, you boys!" Milly exclaimed. "What would any of us do without you?"

"Heaven only knows, Milly," Mrs. Riley said. She turned to Spencer. "Well, we had best get home. Those two girls have been down at the mercantile long enough by themselves."

Clayton flinched. "Oh, no …"

"What?" Spencer asked slowly.

"Well … I sort of told Charlotte Davis that I'd drive her home. She's waiting at the mercantile with Summer and Miss Barstow."

Milly looked at him in shock. "Clayton, whatever possessed you? After what she put you and your wife through?"

"I know, I know," he replied, holding up his hands helplessly.

"Well, a little detour isn't going to hurt anything," Mrs. Riley said in resignation. "Besides, I heard Nellie's not feeling well, so it's not like she'll come bounding out of the house or anything."

Spencer sighed. It was bad enough he had to worry about whether or not Elle fancied him for a husband, but now he'd have to put up with Charlotte's relentless flirting? That Elle would be right there with him probably wouldn't deter Charlotte one bit!

Of course, he could always threaten to arrest her again … "Let's go get it over with, then. The sooner we get home the better. It's getting colder by the minute." He slapped Clayton on the back. "I'll see you tomorrow."

Clayton nodded. "Let Summer know what's going on, all right?" He hugged his mother, then put his arm around Milly.

Spencer escorted his mother back to the mercantile. The wind bit into them and had them both shivering by the time they reached the porch steps. "You go in and warm up while I get the wagon ready," he told her at the door. "Tell Summer and Elle to bundle up nice and tight. It's going to be a cold ride home – and a long one, now that we have to take Charlotte home first."

She nodded and went inside. He went back and prepared the wagon, grabbed the blankets and quilts out of the back, and took them inside the mercantile to warm them before they left.

"Land sakes, it's cold outside!" Mrs. Quinn said as he entered. "Have some coffee before you go home, Spencer."

"Don't mind if I do." He went to the stove first and dropped the blankets down near it. His mother and Summer shook them out and held them near the heat.

Charlotte stood off to one side, staring at the stack of parcels Mrs. Quinn had placed on the front counter – the items purchased for Elle's wedding. Without a word to Charlotte, Spencer went over, gathered them up and headed for the door. "I'll put these in the wagon. As soon as Ma thaws out a bit, let's go."

His mother nodded to him in gratitude as Mrs. Quinn came from the back of the store with a tray of cups, saucers, and a coffee pot. By the time she was done pouring everyone a cup, Spencer had returned. "Gonna be a nippy one tonight," she remarked. "Better make sure your livestock is in the barn, Leona."

"We'll get the stock taken care of just as soon as we get home," Mrs. Riley answered.

"How do you stand it?" Elle asked of Summer. She was shivering just holding the freezing blankets up near the stove to warm them. "I don't think it ever got this cold in New Orleans!"

"This is the coldest it's been since I got here. I'm still not used to it."

Charlotte smirked at them and sipped her coffee, then looked around. "Where's Clayton?"

"He's spending the night at the Browns'," Spencer said. He took a long swallow of the steaming brew. It was hot, and felt good going down.

It *was* cold out, the coldest it had been in years. He looked at the heavy shawl Charlotte had wrapped around her. As much as he didn't like her sometimes – and didn't trust her at *any* time – he couldn't let her walk home in this weather. As it was, they would have to hurry if he was to get her home first and still see to his own family. "Let's go – if it starts to snow, we'll have just that much harder a time of it."

He immediately checked on Elle, figuring that out of everyone, she would be affected the most by the temperature. Above all else, he didn't want her to suffer if she got too chilled. There was a logical remedy for that ... but they had to be married first for them to apply it ...

Longing cut across his heart as he stared at his future bride. She looked back at him, her teeth chattering, and blushed. He turned away suddenly. If he didn't get them all home soon, it wouldn't matter how hotly he gazed at her – it wouldn't be enough in this cold to keep her warm!

He thanked Mrs. Quinn for the coffee, made sure the women were bundled up as best they could, then hurried them all out to the wagon. He helped his mother up onto the wagon seat, then got the others settled in the wagon bed. Summer and Elle pulled the quilts about them. Charlotte, huddled between them, said nothing, only frowned.

"What's the matter, Charlotte?" Elle asked.

"Well, one would think as I'm getting out first that I'd be up front."

"Now, that wouldn't be proper, would it?" Summer asked pointedly. "You up there with another woman's fiancé?"

"But I've known the Riley men nearly all my life. Much longer than either of you."

Summer stiffened beneath the quilts. *The nerve!* "Well, if it's any consolation, you'll be warmer back here between Elle and me," she replied, as coldly as the wind blowing past them.

Charlotte harrumphed in indignation and burrowed deeper into the covers.

With a slap of the reins, they were off. None of the women spoke as the wagon rolled across the frozen ground toward the Davises' place. Spencer worried the women were all but freezing in the back of the wagon as his mother huddled against him for warmth. The temperature was dropping fast – he had to get them all home quickly.

When they reached Charlotte's house Mr. Davis came running – well, waddling – out the door. "Charlotte, where have you been?! Abbey's been home for almost two hours!"

"Nowhere, Daddy," she said flatly.

"I know you were in town, but really! It's freezing out here! You could've caught your death if you'd walked all the way! What were you thinking?" He turned to Spencer. "Thank you for seeing her home, Mr. Riley. I can't thank you enough."

"No problem," Spencer said, then looked a dagger in Charlotte's direction. Clayton had told she'd purposely stayed behind in town to flirt and finagle a ride from one of them. Unfortunately for the Rileys – and fortunately for Charlotte, who would have never made it home on her own dressed as she was – it worked.

Spencer got down, helped her out of the wagon and presented her to her father. He took her by the arm and began pushing her toward the house. "You make it home safe now, you hear?" he told Spencer.

"We will. Keep warm tonight, Mr. Davis – it's gonna be a cold one!"

Mr. Davis shivered, took one look at the dark grey sky, yelled back "it already is!" and quickly went inside, shoving a silent Charlotte ahead of him.

Spencer clambered back up into the wagon and headed straight home. Once there, he knew he'd have to get the women inside, take care of the horses and the livestock, then try and gather enough wood for the fires. It was going to be a long, cold night.

He wished he could spend it with Elle Barstow tucked snuggly in his arms. It was the kind of night that could make any man or woman alone in the world long for a mate. Nor would it be the first time he himself had done so – he had secretly wished for a wife plenty of times. But this time there would a beautiful woman just down the hall from him. Not downstairs – with the temperature dropping, it would be warmer up on the second floor. And with Clayton elsewhere, he was going to suggest to Summer and Elle that they share a bed tonight to stay warm.

How difficult was it going to be for him, though, with Elle just feet away in the next room, and yet untouchable? The deep longing that had begun earlier in the day was widening and deepening fast. Loneliness on a cold winter's night was the worst sort there was.

Spencer looked over his shoulder at the top

of Elle's bonnet. It was all he could see of her, huddled beneath the quilts next to Summer. And for the first time since Clayton and Summer had married, he felt a sharp stab of jealousy. But he knew there was a remedy to both his envy and his loneliness: marriage. And he'd best see to it right away.

NINE

By the time they got back to the farm, Elle was so cold she couldn't feel her toes. Getting out of the wagon took a great effort, and she had to ask Summer to help her stand up. Every fiber of her body was shivering fiercely as she stood waiting for Spencer to help his mother down before seeing to Summer and herself. For their own part, Mrs. Riley and Summer each ran straight for the house as soon as their feet touched the ground.

The wind was picking up, howling through the apple orchards. The grey branches of the trees reminded Elle of bare bones. She shook as she reached down to Spencer's outstretched hands. He grabbed her around the waist and lifted her from the wagon. When her own feet touched the ground, pain shot up her legs, but she still couldn't feel her toes.

"Let's get you inside!" Spencer yelled above the wind as he pulled her close and headed for the farmhouse. She allowed him to keep her wrapped in one arm until they were safely inside.

"Land sakes, it's almost as bad inside as outside!" Mrs. Riley cried from the kitchen. "I need to heat up the stove! Spencer, do you need help in the barn?"

"I should be fine, Ma." He turned to Elle. "You and Summer should get into the kitchen. It'll be the warmest room in the house until we get some fires going."

"How can I help?" Elle asked.

Spencer looked at her and smiled. "You can stay warm; that's the most important thing. But if you really want to help, can you start a fire in the parlor?" He reached up and touched one of her red cheeks with the back of his cold finger. "I'll get more wood after I take care of the horses. We're going to need a lot of it tonight."

Elle swallowed. His finger was freezing, yet his touch set her skin on fire. "Hurry back," she whispered before she could stop herself.

He closed the distance between them and looked into her eyes. "I will." He lingered there, continuing to gaze at her.

Elle was warming up rapidly as she watched him watch her. It was a strange thing to do, and she'd never done it before – just looking at each other, taking each other in ...

Finally Spencer looked away and broke the spell. Elle almost fell forward, as if being pulled by his gaze. "I'd best go see to those horses," he said quietly as he turned. "Get the fire in the parlor going. "I'd like to be able to enjoy it after supper… with you."

She gasped at his words.

He turned back at the sound and again looked

into her eyes. "Elle …," he rasped.

She stared up at him, mesmerized. She'd never seen such a look on someone's face before, and marveled at the power of it. His eyes, the set of his jaw, everything around him seemed suddenly charged with … with …

"Oh my …" was all she managed to say before he took her in his arms and did the one thing she wanted – and dreaded – above all else.

He kissed her.

Usually, a kiss by a handsome man would be welcomed by a young miss, especially if said miss had been hankering after the handsome man to begin with. But Elle Barstow was afraid of a kiss by such a man, and especially this man! She knew, *knew* that it could be her undoing. She'd never been kissed before, by any man, and knew deep down that *this* kiss by *this* man would surely brand her.

And it did. She could feel it in the deepest part of her heart, in the pit of her stomach, and in a couple of places farther south. It did.

He pulled away, his eyes dark with desire, his breath shuddering … and without a word turned to the door and left the house. Left standing in the cold foyer, staring after him, she raised a hand to her lips and touched her mouth. Her lips were warm from the kiss and tingling from having his mouth on hers.

Glorious.

Wonderful.

Incredible.

What other words were there to describe what just happened? She was sure there were plenty, and was tempted to invent a few besides …

"I need some wood!" Mrs. Riley called from the kitchen.

Reality crashed in on Elle like a snow pack falling off a tree branch. Of course, wood. Mrs. Riley needed to keep the fire in the cook stove going, and Elle needed to build another one in the parlor as Spencer had asked.

She looked at the front door and smiled. Her future husband was out there. She touched her lips again. *My future husband, the man I came out here to marry, just* kissed *me* … Her smile deepened.

"Land sakes, where is all my kindling?" Mrs. Riley asked as she came down the hall. "Elle? Elle, are you all right?"

Elle turned to her. "Yes. I'll get you some wood," she replied without thinking and went straight for the front door.

"Be careful, dear – it's frightfully cold out there! Use the wheelbarrow if you need to!"

Elle stepped out onto the front porch and was immediately taken aback by the icy wind. She wrapped her arms around herself and headed for the woodshed near the barn, sure that everything she needed would be there. She'd bring in a load of kindling first, then go back for some bigger pieces. The thought that she would be saving Spencer some trouble fueled her efforts to fight the wind and cold that beat against her and slowed her steps.

But by the time she finally reached the woodshed, she was once again shivering like a struck bell. She got the wheelbarrow, maneuvered it to the woodpile, and began to load it with the kindling they would need, plus a few split logs. Straining, she lifted and pushed her load back toward the house –

– and almost ran down Spencer, returning from the barn. "What are you doing out here?" he yelled at her over the wind. "You'll catch your death!"

"Your mother needed kindling! I offered to come get some," she managed to yell back between teeth chatterings.

He gently moved her away from the barrow, took it the rest of the way to the house and dumped the contents next to the back porch. "I'll get another load – you hurry and get that into the kitchen."

She smiled; he was still going to let her help. She gathered what wood she could into her arms to take into the house, feeling a deeper satisfaction than she'd ever felt before.

Elle dropped the first load into a large bucket Mrs. Riley kept near the stove, then went back outside to get more. Before she was done carrying all of it in, Spencer had returned with a second barrow full. Rather than dump it, he loaded her arms with wood, grabbed an armful of his own, and they carried it into the house. They repeated the process once more before he was satisfied they had enough wood to see them through to the morning. Then he went back to the barn, and she put the wheelbarrow back in the woodshed.

They met again on the way back to the

house. He took her icy hand in his, gave it a
healthy squeeze, and she looked up at him and
smiled. The satisfaction she'd felt earlier at
helping him bring in wood engulfed her heart.
Together they'd performed a simple task, but
one that brought them closer in a profound way.
She couldn't begin to describe how, it just had.
Maybe because it had to do with basic survival,
the need to stay warm, or maybe because she
knew she was helping him, working alongside
him to achieve a goal. Whatever it was, she
liked it, and wanted to experience it again.

It was getting even colder, and the sky was
heavy with black clouds. The smell of snow was
in the air and her lungs strained for breath as she
worked to keep up with him. But none of it
mattered, only the man beside her.

"Let's get inside – you must be half-frozen
by now!" Spencer said as he opened the
kitchen's back door and ushered her through.

The warm air hit Elle in the face and made
her cheeks tingle. She began to shiver and, after
a few failed attempts to remove her coat, found
she couldn't stop.

"Here, let me help you," Spencer said, and
pulled her coat off. He'd already removed his
own, and slung hers over the back of a chair
next to his. Without warning, he pulled her over
by the kitchen stove and drew her into his arms.

She gasped at the action and immediately
tried to pull away, but he wouldn't let her.
"Stop, it's all right. You're freezing and you
need to get warm. Heavens, your hands are
almost blue! Now stand here with me in front of

the stove."

Elle glanced at her hand and, sure enough, it did look a bit bluish. She stopped fighting, and tucked her head beneath his chin, her ear against his broad chest. She could hear his heartbeat and marveled at the sound. She'd never heard a man's heart before … probably because she'd never been this close to a man before! "Isn't this … improper?" she had to ask.

"Not when we're to be married. Besides, it's rather nice, don't you think?"

Elle closed her eyes tightly. Oh, she thought, it was well beyond "nice." If it got any nicer, she wouldn't just defrost – she'd melt into a puddle right there on the floor! How was she going to avoid him now? He'd kissed her! He was holding her! They'd brought in wood together, for heaven's sake! It wasn't a marriage license, but as far as her heart's reaction, it was pretty close. Definitely, something between them had been changed by his kiss, by the work outside, by standing in his arms in front of the cook stove.

And where were Summer and Mrs. Riley? Why weren't they in the kitchen? It was by far the warmest room in the house at the moment. Had they vacated the room on purpose, to give her and Spencer a moment to themselves?

Elle knew that if she didn't get away from him, her resolve to protect her heart until she heard from Mrs. Ridgley would be dashed to pieces. But she couldn't bring herself to pull away. His arms held her as tightly as chains, as firmly as a blood oath. Even if he removed them, though, she knew she would still be just as bound to him.

She realized there might be no turning back – for her heart, that is. Spencer Riley had captured it.

What had he been thinking? He'd kissed Elle! Not a bad thing, mind you, not at all … but up until then he hadn't been sure. The moment he'd run out the door and the cold wind hit him, he should have snapped out of it and had the livestock on his mind. But not with the taste of her sweet mouth lingering on his. Face it, he realized, there was no way his horse could compare with kissing Elle Barstow!

But had *she* been ready for it? Sure, she didn't protest, but he hadn't exactly given her a chance to. She didn't bite him, or step on his foot, or slap him, so that was encouraging … but she didn't say *anything* – not even after he got back and helped her with the wood. A sigh of contentment, a slight swoon, a buckling of the knees, *something* to indicate she'd enjoyed it as much as he did would have helped. All he remembered was her shocked mumble of "Oh God" right before he kissed her. *Oh God* … that could be interpreted a lot of ways, good or bad.

Which of course made him wonder … should he kiss her again? His heart warmed at the thought.

As he was musing on that, Elle pulled away

and stared at the stove for a moment before turning her attention back to him. "What are you smiling about?"

"Nothing, really," he said then gave her waist a small squeeze. "Except this."

She swallowed and quickly looked at the stove again.

He hooked a finger under her chin and pulled it up to so she'd have to look at him. His eyes began to roam her face. "Are you warming up?"

She swallowed again. "Uh-huh ...," she said softly.

Her mouth was perfect; it was all he could do not to taste it again. He licked his lips and closed his eyes. He wanted her like he'd never wanted anything before in his life. She was beautiful, smart, strong – and if things worked out right, in a matter of days she'd be his.

How long *did* it take to sew a wedding dress? And was one really necessary?

"Where ... where do you suppose the others are?" Elle whispered, pulling him from his thoughts.

"I have no idea. Upstairs, perhaps? Ma has a fireplace in her room. Maybe she and Summer are trying to get a fire going up there." His head bent lower, his finger still hooked beneath her chin.

She made a small movement with her head, as if trying to turn away yet not really wanting to.

He cupped her face with his hand to hold her in place and bent his head lower. "Are you okay now?" he whispered.

Her breath hitched and she shivered. "I … I …"

Spencer drew her closer and kissed her again. But this was not the chaste kiss of the front hall. Now he savored his future bride – and to his sheer delight, she slowly returned the favor. She was obviously inexperienced, and he quickly guessed that the one he'd given her in the front hall had been her first.

Tentatively, she pulled one arm from between them and wrapped it around his neck, entwining her fingers in his hair. He deepened the kiss in response.

After a minute he gently drew away from her and stood to his full height. Elle's hand was still in his hair, and he reached up and pulled it from him to place it at her side. "Well…," he said nervously, "I don't know about you, darling, but I'm … quite warm now. We'd best go get a fire going in the parlor. Ma and Summer should be down soon."

She looked up at him, tears in her eyes.

Spencer frowned. What had he done wrong? "Is everything all right, sugar?"

Elle let out a sob, shook her head, pushed away and fled the kitchen, running straight up the stairs. He listened as a door slammed shut, most likely Summer's, then heard a raised voice, also Summer's.

His shoulders sagged. *Spencer Patrick Riley, you beef-brained lout! What did you just do?!*

A moment later came the sound of angry footsteps descending the stairs. His mother. "Spencer! You'd better have a good explanation!" she declared as she reached the bottom.

He tried to speak but nothing came out. He slumped again in dejection, and raised his hands helplessly.

"If you mess this up so help me … oh, just apologize for whatever it was you said to that poor girl!"

"I didn't *say* anything!"

His mother took a step back and looked at him, her face in shock. "What did you do?" she asked in a low, accusing voice.

"All I did was kiss her … she … she didn't stop me …"

Ma Riley crossed her arms over her chest. "If that's all you did, then why in heaven's name is she so upset?"

"Upset? I don't know why! I thought it was okay … she seemed to also ..."

"Then why on earth did she come running up the stairs and tell us she can't marry you?"

His face fell in shocked despair. "What?" he squeaked.

"Those were her exact words! 'I. Can't. Marry. Spencer.'"

TEN

"Elle, what is wrong? What did Spencer do?"

Elle sniffed back her tears. What did Spencer do? There was nothing wrong with what Spencer did! There was *everything* wrong with what she'd done, or not done in this case.

She was going to have to tell him, that was clear. She would never be able to keep what happened in New Orleans to herself while waiting for Mrs. Ridgley's response, not without alienating Spencer and who knows how many other people. It was one thing to hear Spencer talk of honesty between them, but quite another to feel it emanating from him being as he kissed her in the kitchen. Spencer Riley was a good, honest man, true to his word. He deserved better than to be kept in the dark. And if that meant he wouldn't marry her, well, then that was the risk she had to take …

"Oh, Summer! I've done such a terrible thing!"

Summer sat on the bed next to Elle and wrapped her arms around her. "What happened?"

"He kissed me! He kissed me and it was… it was wonderful!"

Summer pulled back and looked at her in confusion. "What's so terrible about that?"

Elle shook her head. "No, you don't understand! Before I came out here, something happened, something awful! I couldn't tell him – I couldn't tell anyone!"

"We are talking about Spencer, aren't we? The kissing part, I mean?"

"Yes … no … I mean, yes, Spencer kissed me! But that's the problem! I can't marry Spencer, he deserves better than …"

Summer took Elle by the shoulders and gave her a shake. "What are you *talking about?*"

Elle looked her square in the eye. "I … I kind of … well, I may have …"

Summer leaned toward her, eyes intense. "You did what? What have you *kind of, may have* done?"

Elle stiffened, closed her eyes tight, and spit it out. "I shot someone."

Summer's mouth hung open for several seconds before she could get it working again. "You did … what?!"

Elle opened her eyes, put a hand to her mouth, and did her best to stifle a sob as she suddenly stood and began to pace about the room. "It all happened so fast, I was running and Jethro kept pushing me and then I tripped and then this man…" Her words poured out like water. She suddenly stopped and turned to Summer. "He was a very *bad* man! I want to stress that!"

Summer stared at her in open-mouthed shock. "Elle," she said gently. "Tell me the part about when you shot him."

Elle twisted a section of her skirt in her hands. "He shot Jethro first."

"Jethro …" Summer whispered, then covered her own mouth in recollection. "I remember Jethro! He works for Mrs. Ridgley!"

Elle nodded as she twisted a section of her skirt in her hands and resumed pacing. "Jethro said the man chasing us probably worked for someone called Slade."

"Slade? Oh no!"

"I don't know who he is, but Jethro told me he was bad, *very* bad. He sent a man after us when we left the orphanage for the train station. He chased us and … and he shot Jethro when we were trying to get out of an alley. He fired as soon as he entered the alley, Jethro went down, then he started walking toward us, like he wasn't in any sort of a hurry. I knew I couldn't leave Jethro with him – he was either going to shoot him dead or let him bleed out! I had to do something!"

Summer's face calmed as she stared into the fire she and Mrs. Riley started in the hearth earlier. "And so you shot him …"

"Yeah," Elle whimpered.

Summer lifted her hands to her temples and began to rub them. "Let me get this straight. Mr. Slade sent someone after you to keep you from getting on that train and bring you back to him. The man he sent chased you into an alley, and shot Jethro, and … wait, where did you get the gun?"

"From Jethro's holster."

Summer nodded absently. "And then you shot the man."

Elle took a deep breath. "Yes."

Summer took her hands from her temples and placed them in her lap. "So ... how does this make you unable to marry Spencer?"

Elle sat down next to her friend. "Don't you see? When I tell Spencer what happened, how could he marry me? He's the sheriff! I ... I don't even know if that man lived or died. I don't know what happened to Jethro!"

"So that's why you were so adamant about getting to the telegraph office," Summer said, staring into the fire.

Elle sighed. "Yes! I was hoping to find out from Mrs. Ridgley what happened before I consented to marry Spencer. I didn't want this hanging over my head and ... and I tried to keep my distance, I tried to avoid feeling anything for him ... in case ..." She dropped her face into her hands and started sobbing in earnest.

Summer put an arm around her friend and waited for the crying to pass. When it did, she said, "Elle, you said yourself Spencer's an honest man. Don't you think he'd listen to you, just as I am? You obviously shot that man in self-defense. Even if he is dead, you're no criminal."

Elle shook her head. "But I left Jethro there. I mean, he told me to run, but still ... I don't know what happened to him! What if he died because of me? He told me to run straight to the train station …"

"Was anyone else there? Did anyone else see what happened?"

"There were … other men coming … I didn't see them, but I could hear them. They must have heard the shots. Jethro and I heard them getting closer and that's when he told me to run. I don't know if they were more of Slade's men, or men who would help, or...." All out of breath, she slumped into Summer's arms.

Summer whistled and shook her head in wonderment. "We'll find out what happened, don't you fret. And don't fret about Spencer either. Telling him is the right thing to do. He'll love you all the more for your honesty."

Elle sobbed against Summer's hair. "You sure? He … he won't arrest me?"

"No, silly, he's not going to arrest you."

Elle sat up and looked at Summer. "I'm so glad you're here. I'd never be able to get through this if you weren't."

"Well, we've been getting each other out of jams since we were little – I don't see any reason to stop now. But I will tell you this – the Riley men are good, honest men, and they'll always do right by you. Give them a chance to prove it. I'm glad I did."

Elle sniffed back the last of her tears. "I will."

Summer smiled, "Good." She again pulled Elle into her arms and hugged her.

The next morning Elle came downstairs with a determined gleam in her eye. She'd spent the night in Summer's room, as it had a fireplace and was much warmer than the one she usually occupied downstairs near the kitchen. That was an office Clayton and Spencer had converted into a bedroom for Summer when she arrived with her injured foot, and they'd left it as one knowing Elle was on her way.

She entered the kitchen, went to the stove and poured herself a cup of coffee. Summer had come down earlier and started on breakfast. She was standing next to the stove frying eggs. "Good morning, Elle."

Elle smiled at her friend and confidante. "Can I help with anything?"

"You could slice some bread."

Elle went to the breadbox, got out a loaf, took a knife, and went to it. "Where's Spencer?"

"Out at the barn. He should be in any minute. Are you going to tell him this morning?"

Elle stopped her slicing. "I'm not sure. I want to, but think I should wait for the right moment."

"Don't wait any longer than you have to, is my advice." Summer smiled, then turned back to the eggs. "I'm glad you told me first."

"Why?"

"I don't know … because we've always told each other everything, I suppose. It won't be the same when we're both married – I suppose we'll be telling all our secrets to Clayton and Spencer first."

Elle put the bread on a plate and set it on the table, secretly praying that she was still *going* to get married! The voice of doubt had whispered to her all night that once Spencer found out what she'd done, their wedding would be off. No happy ending to her tale of woe, no pretty wedding dress or flower-strewn altar – just a cold jail cell, a view of Spencer's back as he walked away, and then a long ride in chains back to Louisiana to face her fate. It even showed her the newspaper headline: 'ORPHAN GIRL KILLER SENTENCED TO HANG!' She'd hardly slept a wink.

The back door to the kitchen suddenly opened, letting a chill into the room. Spencer stomped his boots on a small rug to get the fresh snow off before looking up into Elle's eyes. "Good morning," he said as he took off his coat and hat and hung them on a peg near the door. "Is breakfast ready?"

Elle had frozen, staring back, her heart in her throat.

"Sit down and I …," Summer began, then suddenly stopped. "And *Elle* will fix you a plate," she finished. She looked Elle in the eye and silently mouthed, *tell him!*

Elle glared at her just as Spencer turned around and headed for the nearest chair. She went to the stove and dished him up some fried eggs and potatoes as Summer placed a plate of bacon on the table.

"Thank you, Miss Barstow," he told her as she set his breakfast plate in front of him.

She sighed at the way he addressed her. After

the way he kissed her last night, it was back to Miss Barstow now? But then, Mrs. Riley *had* heard her say she couldn't marry him ... she must have told him as much. What if he decided that was fine and dandy? Worse, what if he decided to send her back?!

Elle stood behind him and raised her face to the ceiling in silent prayer. *Lord, what a mess I've created! Make this work out, because ...* She looked at Spencer and watched as he bowed his head over his plate in a silent prayer of his own before he dug into his breakfast. *Because, Lord, I don't dare go back! And even if I did, I can't leave him. I ... I think I'm falling in love with him!*

But did he feel anything for her at this point? And if he did, would he after she told him what she'd done?

Summer walked by her and snapped her with a dishrag to get her attention, then motioned with her head as if to say *do it already, will you?*

Elle shook her head in fear. *Not now!* she mouthed back.

Summer gave her a warning glare, then began to dish herself up a plate.

Elle put a hand to her forehead and began to massage it. She couldn't tell him over breakfast – let the poor man eat. She'd tell him when he was done. Yes, that's what she'd do ... just as soon as he was done ...

The front door suddenly opened and closed. Spencer's head snapped up at the sound and he stood up from the table. "Clayton, is that you?"

"It sure is," Clayton said as he strolled into the kitchen. "Where's my lady?"

Summer turned to him and smiled. He went directly to her, pulled her into his arms, and kissed her soundly.

Elle felt a tremendous blush creep into her cheeks, and she had to look away. Not because of the way Clayton was kissing Summer, but because it brought up the memory of the kisses she'd shared with Spencer last night. Her whole body shivered just thinking about it.

"How's Doc doing?" Spencer asked.

"He's awake. He finally stirred about three o'clock this morning. Always was an early riser!"

"Thank the Lord!" Spencer said in relief. "What about Milly?"

"She's fine – plumb tuckered out, but fine. Mrs. Quinn showed up with some muffins and coffee and took over my watch. She was nagging Milly something awful when I left."

"That's good news," Summer agreed. "About Doc, I mean, not the nagging."

"Where's Ma?" Clayton asked as he looked around the kitchen.

"Right here, dear," Mrs. Riley said as she bounced into the room in her usual cheery manner. She went straight to Clayton. "Doc Brown?"

"He'll be fine. Got a nasty bump on the side of his head, and he says his vision's a little fuzzy, but he thinks it'll clear up by tomorrow."

"Milly'll most likely make him stay in bed at least that long," Mrs. Riley speculated. "The poor man. It's certainly hard to be treated by the doctor after an accident like that when you *are* the doctor!"

"You can say that again," Clayton exclaimed as he stole some bacon off of Spencer's plate. "Milly's sure no peach when she's in the role." He took a bite and ignored Spencer's scowl.

"I'm afraid Doc and Milly aren't getting any younger," Mrs. Riley added. "Matthew Quinn is going to have some mighty big shoes to fill!"

"Matthew Quinn?" Spencer began. "What does he have to do with anything?"

"Didn't you know? He's coming home from college soon," Mrs. Riley said happily.

"Yes, but what does that have to do with Doc and Milly?" Clayton asked.

"Now you boys should both remember! Matthew went to school to become a doctor!"

Clayton's brow furrowed. "I thought he went to school to learn how to run his parent's mercantile."

"Why would he go all the way to Boston to learn *that*? No, our Matthew will come back to Nowhere and help out Doc Brown – that's the plan!"

"The plan?" Summer asked, curious now about the subject.

"Well, he can't very well expect to start his own practice while Doc Brown is still working!" said Mrs. Riley. "No one will want to see him so fresh out of school! Besides, I'm not sure Nowhere is big enough to support *two* doctors' offices!"

"Well, I'll be, Ma – you're right," Spencer

said as he grabbed more bacon from the plate on the table. "How did I forget that?"

Elle listened to the conversation. It was homey in a way – their talk of the townsfolk, Doc Brown and his wife Milly, Matthew Quinn coming home – and made her feel like she belonged there. She'd learned quite a lot about some of the townsfolk just by listening to the Rileys! She would be happy to spend the rest of her life here on this farm, with the town of Nowhere a few miles away. By a miracle she'd been reunited with her best friend, and was happy Summer had married into such a wonderful family …

… but a big question mark still hung over all her hopes.

Elle sighed to herself as she went to stand next to the stove. It was bad enough having to think about what Spencer would do when she told him what happened in New Orleans. Imagine what someone like Charlotte Davis might do with the news. She'd be branded a murderer by the time that girl was done with her. Then the whole town would shun her, and Spencer's reputation as sheriff would be tainted – if he got to remain sheriff ...

She closed her eyes against the pain the thought caused. She couldn't stand it if such a thing happened to Spencer! He shouldn't have to suffer for her wrongs!

She knew she had to tell him – and she would. But the more she thought about it, the more she knew she still would not be able to marry him. Eventually the gossips in town would find out. Spencer would have to investigate it. It was a small town after all, not a big city like New Orleans where secrets were more easily kept.

What on earth was she going to do? How could she protect Spencer's reputation?

A thought suddenly came to her. It hurt … but it made sense. What if she were to simply leave?

She could get a ticket for the stage, at least to the next town, and start a life there. Going back to Louisiana was out of the question, but going elsewhere wasn't. She was sure Summer would help her. As soon as she got to wherever she was going, she could find a job and get settled. Spencer and Mrs. Riley wouldn't be out any money; she could easily pay them back from her earnings. It could work. She'd tell Spencer the whole story, and then leave immediately with no harm – or no further harm – done.

The thought of Charlotte Davis lamenting over becoming a spinster flashed through her mind. Elle turned to the stove and poked at the fried potatoes. Charlotte wasn't the only one looking at that possibility. The girl might be a pill, a gossip and a liar, but at least she hadn't done anything in her past that could destroy an innocent family's reputation and get her hung by the neck until dead.

Tears burned Elle's eyes as she turned again and watched the Rileys continue talking about this and that. She suddenly felt like a complete outsider, whereas a minute ago she, for a brief moment at least, had felt like she belonged here.

That is, until she realized the damage to Spencer's reputation her deeds could bring.

And what made it all the worse was that she knew she wasn't falling in love with Spencer Riley. She was already there.

ELEVEN

Spencer could *feel* Elle behind him as she stood near the stove. Her lovely presence permeated the room and filled him with peace and calm. How could he possibly let her go? He couldn't – *wouldn't* – do it!

Regardless of what his mother had told him last night, he was determined to find out what was wrong with his future bride. It was only a kiss! Well, okay, it was two, but that wasn't reason to cancel a wedding! It's not like there was anything improper about them. Most couples kissed before they were married; why should they be any different?

But just to be safe, and in the hope it would make her feel better, he'd addressed her as "Miss Barstow" a few moments ago instead of "Elle." It hadn't seemed to help.

"You know, when Matthew returns, he'll automatically become the most eligible bachelor in town!" his mother exclaimed, snapping him out of his thoughts.

"Just about the *only* eligible bachelor in town," Clayton laughed.

"Now, Clayton! You know Billy Blake's not married yet …"

"Yet. He and Abbey Davis are just about joined at the hip."

"And then there's that handsome new deputy in town!" his mother added.

"True, but there aren't a lot of unattached females of age in town either," Spencer pointed out, then turned to look at Elle. She stood straight at his perusal of her, then quickly looked away. He frowned, and had a mind to kiss her again, just to show her she was definitely not among the "unattached."

"Charlotte Davis is unattached," Summer said calmly.

"Charlotte Davis?!" Clayton and Spencer squawked in unison. Both men looked at her as if her face had sprouted a third eye.

Summer shrugged. "Yes, I know she drives everyone crazy, myself included. And her character has been … questionable. But even Charlotte deserves a chance at love."

"I agree," Elle said.

Everyone turned to look at her.

Elle swallowed hard before she squared her shoulders. "After all, there are a lot worse things than being a gossip and a flirt."

"Like what?" Spencer asked.

Elle's eyes widened at his remark and she took a step back. "There … just are ..."

Spencer noticed how Summer gave Elle a look, then rolled her eyes and turned around again. Hmmm… now what was that about?

"I'm afraid I'll have to disagree with you

girls. It would take nothing short of a miracle for that girl to change her ways," said Ma Riley.

"Or the right man," Elle whispered.

Spencer wasn't sure if the others had heard her, but he had. He got up from the table and went over to her. He wanted to settle things now, before he had to go to work – he did *not* want to spend the day twisting in the wind, wondering if Elle wanted to marry him.

She watched him approach and tried to take another step back, but he grabbed her before she backed into the hot stove. "Be careful!" He didn't mean for it to come out sounding like a scold, but it did.

Her lips formed into a thin line as she looked up at him. Lord, but she was beautiful, even when she was angry! He felt his body grow warm, and it wasn't because of the stove.

"We need to talk," he told her softly.

She turned away briefly, then slowly looked up at him. "I know."

Spencer glanced at the table. Clayton, Summer and his mother were all staring at them in silence. "In the parlor." He took her hand and, ignoring the rest of his family, led her past the kitchen table and into the hall.

Once they were in the parlor, he sat them both down on the settee. "Elle…"

She held up a hand. "I'll make this easy on you. I can't marry you."

He felt his body go cold. It was one thing to suspect how she might feel about him, another to hear it from her own lips. She didn't care for him – why else would she not want to marry him? But … the kisses they'd shared the day before said otherwise.

"Elle, I respect how you feel, but you need to give this a chance. You did sign a contract, and we could have already been married by now. What then?"

She looked at him, and he could see tears forming in her eyes. "I know. It's just that I … I can't marry you."

His heart wrenched at her words. He realized he cared even more for her than he'd thought. How could he let her go? "Elle, I know this might be hard for you, coming all the way out here and being so far from home–"

"Home?" she said, surprised, then quickly looked away. "No … that's not it."

Spencer wanted to kick himself. *What* home? She was an orphan from the same ill-funded establishment Summer had come from. What kind of a home could it be? Certainly not one she was longing to return to.

But then, what *was* the problem? "Elle, what's wrong? Tell me – tell me now."

Her tears finally broke free. "Oh, Spencer … I can't …, I don't want anything to happen to you!"

"What?"

"Spencer?" Summer said from the hall.

He looked up. She and Clayton were standing and watching them, holding hands. The same pang of jealousy he'd felt the day before struck him again. He turned back to Elle as they stepped into the parlor, their mother close behind.

Clayton looked down at Elle and smiled. "We don't want you to leave, Miss Barstow. We discussed it in the kitchen. We're not blind, you know – it's been obvious to all of us that something's wrong. All we can ask is that you give Spencer a chance. This mail-order bride business is just that, a business. You sign a contract, board a train or stage, reach your destination and get married. My brother and I … well, neither of us went about it the conventional way, I admit. We both wanted a little time to get to know our brides first."

"Yours was *anything* but conventional," Spencer pointed out.

Clayton raised his brow at that. "But what happened between Summer and I did serve to give us time to court before we were married."

"Though I wouldn't have minded a different method," Summer said with a laugh.

Clayton nodded and smiled. "You see how it is in this family, Miss Barstow? But even so, Summer and I *are* happily married! And I can look back and happily say that we *came* to be married, in large part, because I shot my bride-to-be in the foot. Now, I can't imagine you've done anything worse than that …"

"*I* shot a man in New Orleans," Elle said.

Everyone's eyes were riveted on her – even Summer, who already knew the story.

Elle looked at them, her face void of emotion. "But I don't think I'll ever be able to say it *happily* to anyone – least of all a man I'm supposed to marry."

Spencer heard Summer sigh in relief, but was too paralyzed to react. He was frozen, eyes locked on Elle as if she had just drawn a gun on *him*. He tried desperately to gather his wits after her sudden declaration. "What … what did you say?" he asked haltingly.

"You heard me," Elle told him, trying not to choke up as she looked at his shocked face. She certainly hadn't planned on telling him like that – the words were out before she knew it, and it was too late to take them back. Just like she hadn't planned to grab Jethro's gun. Just like she couldn't take that bullet back.

"What happened?" Spencer asked firmly as he got up, stood in front of her and took her hands in his. "Tell me everything."

Clayton pulled a chair closer and sat, his eyes intent on Elle. Summer went to stand behind him. Mrs. Riley, half in shock, fell onto the closest piece of furniture, a rocking chair near the window.

Elle swallowed hard and looked at Summer who offered the barest of nods in return. She took a deep breath. "I shot a man because he was chasing me… while I was on my way to the train station to come out west ..." And without a pause, she told them the entire story – the chase, the man Slade had sent and why, Jethro, the gun, the money, the long hungry journey, everything.

She was shocked at the unusual calm that had

come over her. Everything had turned surreal, her entire future blurred. She had no idea which direction her life would go from here. She was sitting in a farmhouse parlor with a sheriff and an ex-sheriff, throwing herself on their mercy with nothing but her word to go on.

When she finished, there was silence in the room for a time. Elle swore she could hear the dust pattering on the floor.

Clayton turned in his chair to look at Summer. "Is all this true?"

Summer bit her lower lip and nodded.

"Why didn't you tell me?" Clayton asked. "Is this the reason you were so afraid of having to go back to New Orleans after you arrived? Who are these men?"

"Clayton," Summer interjected. "I'm sorry I didn't tell you about Mr. Slade before."

"It's all right," Clayton responded. "I can understand not wanting to talk about someone like …" He wrinkled his nose in disgust. "… *that*."

"This Slade," Spencer echoed, shaking his head. "People like that exist?!"

"Indeed they do," Summer replied. "Forgive me for being crude, but … I can't imagine any girl would work in a brothel willingly. And not only does he own and operate several, but …." She took a deep breath before continuing. "… I'm told he runs an underground slave ring, buying and selling women and children mostly."

"Oh my Lord, no!" Mrs. Riley gasped, clutching her bodice in consternation. "What a devil!"

"Damnation," Spencer said to himself, his jaw tight. He looked down at Elle, then sat again on the settee and looked her in the face so intensely that she thought she might faint. Her eyes filled with tears. She could sense the immense power emanating from him, and it scared her. Even though she was sure it wasn't directed at her, but the enormity of the situation, it frightened her all the same. She'd never experienced anything like it in her life.

Without warning he grabbed her and held her close. "Elle, Elle, I'm so sorry. You shouldn't have to be afraid to tell me anything, do you hear? Anything at all ..."

A sob of relief escaped as her tears fell. She cried into his broad chest as he held her and kissed the top of her head, rubbing her back with his hand.

"I care about you, do you understand?" he whispered in her ear. "Never, *ever* be afraid to talk to me."

She sucked in a breath. "Wh ... what did you say?" came out a raspy whisper.

He pulled away just far enough to cup her face in his hands. "I said, I care about you. More than words can express. Unless of course those words are ... I love you."

Her eyes went wide, and speech failed her. This was the last thing she'd expected him to say after she'd told him about New Orleans. "You're ... you're not going to arrest me?"

"Good Lord, no!" he laughed. "Why on earth would I do that? Sweetie, you're innocent until proven guilty – and given what you've told me,

I have no reason to believe you're the guilty party in this."

Elle launched herself at Spencer. He held her to him once more and whispered words of comfort to soothe her fears.

Clayton stood and took Summer into his own arms. "You really should have told me."

"I'm sorry. I was frightened, too, and I know what would happen if she had to go back to New Orleans. There's no hope for girls like Elle and me there — not after the war, not with the Slades of the world prowling around. Mrs. Ridgley, she's like an angel and does her best to get us away from there." She glanced over at Elle, who was still wrapped tightly in Spencer's arms.

"What a horror," Mrs. Riley said, then asked Summer, "Are there any other girls about to leave the orphanage?"

Elle answered before Summer could. "There is one about to leave, if she hasn't already – she came from another orphanage that burned down just a few weeks before Summer left. Her name is Sequoia, Sequoia Rose." She sniffled and lifted her head from Spencer's shoulder. "I don't think those bad men know about her."

"Now I know why you were so adamant about getting word to Mrs. Ridgley," Spencer stated.

"Yes – I have to know what happened! I don't know if the man I shot is alive or dead! And Jethro – that man would've killed him for certain if …"

"If you hadn't shot him first?"

She nodded.

Spencer looked up at Clayton. "Sounds like self-defense, pure and simple."

Clayton nodded. "We'd best both go into town and see if there's any word from Mrs. Ridgley. Probably too soon, but one never knows. It'll give me a chance to check on Doc while I'm at it."

Spencer nodded, then noticed their mother pacing back and forth. "Ma, you'll wear a hole in the carpet. Everything's fine now."

She stilled and looked at him, her face red. "If you say so, dear. But if you're going to town, then I've got to come along!"

"Why? You were just there yesterday," Clayton inquired.

"There's something I need to discuss … with Mrs. Quinn."

Spencer gently let go of Elle and stood. "Ma … Ma, I know that look on your face. What are you planning?"

"What do you mean, what am I planning? Your wedding, you silly goose!"

Both men studied her carefully, suspecting there was more to it than that, but unable to prove it. Finally, Clayton said, "Well, that makes sense. I'll go hitch up the horses."

Spencer sighed in relief, took Elle into his arms and looked down into her eyes. "Elle Barstow?"

Elle started at the sound of her name. "Yes?"

"Let's get married."

Elle let loose a squeak of surprise. "You … you mean it?"

"You're supposed to be my bride, aren't you? That's why you're here."

"Well, yes, but I … I thought …"

"Maybe you're thinking a little too much. I'm not letting you weasel out of our contract. We're getting hitched. Now."

"Spencer!" Ma Riley cried. "We haven't made the dress yet!"

"How long will that take?" he countered.

"Give Summer and I a few days, at least!"

He looked at Elle. "I don't know if I can wait that long."

She smiled. Oh, how she loved him in that moment! "We don't have to wait, if you don't want to."

He leaned down and whispered in her ear. "How badly do you need that dress?"

She smiled as a shiver went up her spine. "All I really need is you ..."

"Oh dear heavens … let us make this poor girl her dress and do things properly!" Ma Riley shook her head. "We'll get Abbey Davis to help – we can have it done in two days!"

Elle kept smiling – it was either that or start crying again, though at least these would be tears of joy. Still, she didn't want to do anything to delay Spencer and Clayton from going to town and finding out if Mrs. Ridgley had wired back. "I can wait a few more days if you can."

"Thank you, Elnora," Leona replied quickly. "Glad to see someone's got some sense. Two days it is!"

"I'm outvoted as usual," Spencer groaned. "Fine, two days. But I'm not waiting any longer than that!" He turned back to Elle, looked into her eyes, and forgot about saying anything else. Thankfully, he didn't need words to tell her what he wanted to say. His eyes, his face, the way he stood and held her said it all.

Elle could see clear as day that he loved her, and that this was only the beginning of that love. The thought of having the rest of their lives before them to grow and nurture it was overwhelming! How could she possibly receive such love from another person? As an orphan growing up, she'd craved love and thought she would never get enough of it. But this … this made her realize she'd been thinking on far too small a scale.

To give her a taste of that love, Spencer bent his head to her and kissed her right there, in front of God and his family, like she'd never been kissed before.

TWELVE

The next two days found Elle, Summer, and Abbey scrambling to finish Elle's wedding dress. Mrs. Riley was kept equally busy, seeing to the rest of the wedding preparations.

Elle marveled at Spencer and his family as she worked. Their love and acceptance of her was astounding, and she wished she'd told Spencer of her predicament the moment she'd gotten off the stage. But how could she have known they'd understand? Of course, sometimes you just had to step out and take a risk – but Elle, like Summer, was still learning to do that.

"Elle, you want a longer length of lace off the cuffs? Or should I keep it shorter?" Abbey asked.

"Longer if we have enough – I think it would be much prettier that way," Elle told her. "Thank you so much for volunteering to help. You're a much better seamstress than I am!"

"Or I," added Summer. "Elle and I can patch up just about anything, and handle some simple dresses, but nothing like what you've been doing. We never could have finished this without you."

"Oh, I don't mind," Abbey said brightly. "I love to sew fancy things. In fact, I'll tell you a secret."

Elle and Summer both leaned toward her in anticipation.

"I've already made *my* wedding dress!"

Both girls gasped.

"And after I'm married, I want to have my own dress shop one day, just like Mrs. Jorgensen."

"You would certainly be good at it!" Elle said with a smile. "I wish I was as good at this as you are."

"You already made your wedding dress?" Summer said in astonishment.

"Yes, I did! Mother thinks it was a silly thing to do, but I don't. I ... well, I hope to be married very soon."

Summer and Elle both smiled and nodded. They knew Abbey was deeply in love with Billy Blake. They also knew that Mrs. Davis likely didn't approve of the match.

Abbey turned to Elle. "And don't worry, it just takes practice. After you're married, you can try making a dress for the annual Valentine's dance. We have it every year, and it's a lot of fun!"

"I heard Mrs. Quinn mention it when we were in the mercantile the other day," Summer began. "She made it sound like it was one of the big events of the year."

"Oh, it is!" Abbey told them with a smile.

"There's a dinner and everything! It's as much fun as the Fourth of July celebration. I'm going to start on my dress just as soon as we're done with this one!"

"We can check with Clayton and Spencer, then go back down to the mercantile and pick out some fabrics," Summer said.

"I hate to ask, after all the work you've done the last couple of days, but could you see it in your heart to help us if we need it?" Elle asked as Abbey began to sew lace onto one cuff.

Abbey looked up at her and smiled. "Sure! We can work on our dresses here or at my house. Even Charlotte will be working on one."

"I thought Charlotte usually employed Mrs. Jorgensen to make her dresses," said Summer.

"Not always. In fact, Daddy has been insisting we make more of our own clothing and not rely on Mrs. Jorgensen all the time. I've always loved making mine, but Charlotte doesn't care too much for sewing. She will occasionally make something, and she's actually quite good at it too."

Elle looked to Summer before she spoke. "Do you think your sister would mind having us over to your house to work on our dresses?"

Abbey laughed. "Oh, of course she wouldn't mind. She's not as bad as all that – more bark than bite."

Summer, for obvious reasons, was skeptical. "Yes, well … I've heard her barking, and she could do with a muzzle," she said dryly. "No offense, Abbey, but your sister can be…"

"Difficult?" Abbey finished for her. "You

don't have to tell me – I live with her. But I think she's calming down and joining the rest of the human race. At least I hope she is, or she'll never marry."

"Well, let's not talk about it anymore," Summer said. "This is supposed to be about Elle."

Elle smiled and continued to work on the hem. "Thank you, Summer. You too, Abbey. I still can't believe I'm getting married tomorrow!"

"I hope it's not going to be too cold," Abbey said. "Mother's still not feeling well, and I know she'll want to attend."

Summer visibly stiffened. Elle caught the action and said, "I've not had the pleasure of meeting your mother yet. But I wouldn't want her coming if the cold is going to hamper her healing."

Abbey looked at them both. "I really shouldn't say this, but sometimes I think my mother would like to hamper your wedding!"

Summer let go a snort of laughter. "I'm sorry – I shouldn't laugh at that, but … having met her …" She stifled another chuckle.

"Why would she want to do that?" Elle asked as she set her sewing down and stared at the two of them.

Abbey sighed. "I'm sorry to admit it, but my mother gets these things in her head, and thinks that it should play out exactly as she envisioned. She'd planned for Clayton and Charlotte to get married after Clayton's first wife Sarah passed on. When he married Summer instead, I thought she was going to break a window. Instead she broke her favorite vase."

"Oh dear, no!" Elle said. "What happened?"

"She threw it against a wall. She *said* she dropped it, but she threw it. And Charlotte cried for days of course. Summer, I'll stop talking about it if you want – it can't be much fun for you to hear."

"I'm fine, Abbey. Clayton and I love each other, and I'm not worried about your sister or your mother as far as he's concerned."

"I'm glad to hear that," Abbey said, then sighed again. "Daddy's been patient, but Mother sure is coming down hard on Charlotte to find a *suitable husband*." She said the last part with her nose in the air.

"From what Clayton tells me, there's not many young men around here," Summer said. "He made it sound like Spencer was it as far as eligible bachelors go – except for Billy, of course, but he's taken."

Abbey blushed.

"What about Mrs. Quinn's son? The one coming home early from college?" Elle asked.

"Matthew Quinn – yes, he'll be home in a week or two. Mother is already dropping his name, but Charlotte doesn't seem interested …"

"Charlotte, not interested in an eligible bachelor?" Summer asked incredulously.

Abbey nodded. "I told you – I think she's calming down."

Elle let go a long sigh. "I never realized how hard it was to find a husband! I'm glad I became a mail-order bride!"

"So am I!" added Summer.

"You won't be a bride at all if we don't get this dress done!" Abbey said. "After we finish the cuffs and hem, I'll sew on the rest of the lace, and then let's have you try it on."

Elle giggled with delight. "I can't wait to see what it looks like once it's finished!"

The three continued to work well into the afternoon. Once they had it done to Abbey's satisfaction, they took it upstairs to Clayton and Summer's room, which had a full-length mirror, so they could see how it looked and make any adjustments needed. But as soon as Elle stepped into it and pulled it on, she shivered in anticipation. She still couldn't get over the fact she was going to marry Spencer the very next day!

"Oh, Elle!" Summer exclaimed. "It's beautiful!"

"It's perfect," Abbey whispered.

A knock sounded at the bedroom door. Abbey answered it, and Mrs. Riley came in. "Oh, good heavens, you look positively divine!"

Elle couldn't help it, she began to cry.

"Elle, what's wrong?" Summer asked as Abbey bent to the skirt of the dress to smooth it out.

"I don't know. I guess it's because I've never seen myself look like this before."

Abbey stood and looked at Elle's reflection in the mirror. "You are beautiful, Elle! Hasn't anyone ever told you that?"

Elle thought about it, and realized that in her eighteen years of life, no, nobody had. Cute, maybe. Spunky, spirited … but not beautiful. "No," she said softly, shaking her head.

"Well, Spencer will be telling you! A lot!" Mrs. Riley said with a smile. Then she clapped her hands together. "Oh, I'm going to have a house full of grandchildren in no time!"

Elle's eyes widened. "Let's not rush things!" she quickly replied.

"Why, Elnora – don't you want children?"

Elle wiped a tear away. "Of course – but I'd like to really get to know my husband first."

Mrs. Riley smiled as she headed for the door. "Oh don't worry dear, you will!"

The three girls watched her leave, then burst into giggles, Elle most of all. Tomorrow night, she would be getting to know her husband *quite* well.

The next day the Riley household was abuzz with activity. The wedding was scheduled for after the church service, and Spencer was a nervous wreck knowing half the town planned to stay after and watch him take his vows. He was so shaken, he dropped his tie three times before he had it in his hands long enough to get it around his neck and done up properly.

Clayton sat back and watched his younger brother flit about the bedroom like a caged bird. "For crying out loud, Spence, calm down."

"I can't calm down! I'm getting married!"

Clayton laughed. "You'd think you were

having your first child, the way you're acting."

"If I was having my first child, I don't think I'd be standing at all. Besides, that's Elle's job, having the babies."

Clayton rolled his eyes. "If you don't calm down, you're not going to have any energy left to *make* those babies!"

Spencer stopped in the middle of the room and buttoned his vest. He took a deep breath, then another. "I don't know why I'm so skittish. Maybe it's because everyone in town wants to watch me get married. Not to mention we haven't heard anything from that Mrs. Ridgley yet."

"It's only been a couple of days since Elle sent the message. She didn't get back to me for at least three. Don't worry, once she does we'll get to the bottom of what happened and straighten it out. And so what if everyone in town wants to watch you get married? Quite a few watched me get married, remember?"

Spencer turned to face him. "You were a good sheriff, Clayton. Everyone in town loved having you in the position. They love *you*. I hope I'm able to fill your shoes."

Clayton smiled. "Don't worry, little brother. You've done fine so far."

"I haven't even made an arrest yet as sheriff," Spencer pointed out. "And nothing had better happen at work for the next week or so. I'd like to see to the making of those babies you mentioned earlier without being interrupted by an outlaw or something."

Clayton laughed again. "Now you're

talking!" He stood, crossed the room and slapped his brother on the back. "Well, Sheriff Riley, what say we go get you hitched?"

Spencer smiled, put on his jacket, and the two of them went downstairs.

Billy was waiting for them outside the farmhouse with the wagon. Mr. Quinn had come earlier and taken the women into town and over to the church. The Quinns would be in attendance, of course, along with Doc and Milly (Doc having made good progress), Abbey and the rest of the Davises (even Nellie, who'd also made a speedy recovery), and of course Billy, who wasn't about to let Abbey out of his sight and whom Clayton and Spencer suspected would be married himself soon. *Very* soon if Billy had his way, which meant they would be short another deputy. But they'd deal with that later.

The ride into town was cold, and Spencer worried about Elle's own ride with Mr. Quinn, and the others. He'd been busy looking for his tie when they left, but Clayton assured him that the women would be warm enough during the ride to the church. Elle would change into her wedding dress there. They would have the ceremony, then the wedding party would come back to the farm for a small wedding supper and cake.

Quiet, peaceful, quaint: that's what Spencer had planned for Elle. A nice little wedding amongst close friends and family (okay, so that meant half the town, but he hadn't invited them to supper) with his beautiful bride at his side.

What more could he ask for?

He smiled. This was the first time his mother hadn't given him a scarf and mittens for Christmas. Instead she'd sent away for Elnora Barstow. Looking back, he was glad Ma had made the change.

His grin broadened. Maybe by the end of the year, he and Elle would be giving Ma her first grandchild.

Abbey adjusted Elle's veil. She stood in front of a small mirror in the preacher's office. "You look lovely!"

Elle fidgeted. "I wish I could see myself better."

"You've seen what the dress looks like on you, just not the veil," Summer observed. "Are you ready?"

"Oh, Summer!" Elle turned to her friend. "I'm nervous!"

"So was I – though I have to say, not as much as you are."

Elle grimaced. "Really? Am I being a ninny?"

"Of course not. You have every right to be nervous. The circumstances around my wedding were much different. I had more than just the wedding to worry about when I got married."

Elle stared at her friend a moment. "Is this another story you haven't told me?"

Abbey grimaced. "Is this the one about

staying over at –"

"No, I told her that one. I was thinking about what happened at the stage stop."

"Oh, Lord," Abbey declared, holding her hand to her chest. "Maybe you should hold off on that one until later."

"I think you're right," Summer chuckled.

Elle had been distracted from their conversation by the sound of the townsfolk in the sanctuary, milling about while waiting for the ceremony to get started. "Is it time?"

"Almost." Summer handed her a flower arrangement made of ribbons. "Here, I made it myself. I hope you like it."

Elle looked at the pretty blue silk flowers. "Oh, Summer, it's beautiful. I'd forgotten how you used to make flowers out of ribbons like this. Thank you!"

"There aren't any flowers around here this time of year to pick for a bouquet – well, not any nice ones. So I made you this instead."

Elle hugged her friend.

"Girls!" Mrs. Riley exclaimed as she rushed into the room. "It's wedding time!"

Elle froze for a second while Summer and Abbey quickly set about adjusting Elle's dress one last time. They followed Mrs. Riley to the door.

Clayton was waiting there for them. "I'd be honored to give you away, if that's all right with you," he told Elle.

"Oh my goodness, I hadn't even thought of that!" she whispered as the church began to quiet down. Music began to play. It was the introduction of the wedding march.

Elle sucked in a breath. "Oh my …"

"This is it," Summer told her in an excited whisper. "At last, we'll be sisters for real!"

Elle looked to her and smiled. "Oh, Summer, I'm so happy I could cry!"

"You'll cry when you see Spencer," Clayton chuckled as he held his arm out to her.

The music changed, and Elle quickly took his arm. Even she recognized this as the part where she was to walk down the aisle. "Why?"

Clayton positioned them at the end of the aisle and looked over at her. "Because, Miss Barstow, he's going to make you the best husband you could ever wish for."

Elle looked to the end of the aisle where Spencer stood next to the preacher. The music played, the townspeople smiled, and Elnora Barstow walked down the aisle to stand next to her future husband. This was it! This was the moment she'd imagined in the secret places of her mind, the place where the impossible dreams were all kept, the ones she thought might never come true.

But this one was.

Clayton was right – when she stood before Spencer Riley and looked into his eyes she did indeed cry. And for more than one reason. First, because the love that shone in his eyes was undeniable. She marveled that he could have such love for her in so little time. If this was the beginning, how much will it have grown five, ten, twenty years from now?

And second …

"Sheriff Riley!"

All heads turned as Tom Turner came stumbling into the church, completely out of breath. He suddenly stopped and bent over, his hands on his knees, trying to catch his breath from his sprint through town.

"Deputy, what's the meaning of this?!" Clayton snapped. "Can't you see we're in the middle of a wedding?"

Tom made his way down the aisle, his breathing still ragged, and pulled a piece of paper from his vest pocket.

Clayton stepped out in front of him and blocked his path. "I'll take that."

"I'm sorry, Mr. Riley, but this here's official business, an' – beggin' your pardon, sir – yer no longer sheriff."

Clayton turned to Spencer and shrugged helplessly.

Spencer quickly glanced to Elle, who was in as much shock as everyone else. "What is it, Tom?"

"This just came for ya, sheriff. I thought ya better read it right away." He stole a quick glance at Elle. "By the way ... congratulations on yer weddin'."

Spencer nodded to him as he took the note. It was from the telegraph office. He quickly read it, and could feel the blood draining from his face. "Oh, good God ..."

"Spencer?" Elle asked softly. "Spencer, what is it?"

He looked to her, his face frozen with shock. "Elle ... Elle, I'm so sorry."

She took a shuddering breath, eyes wide. "Sorry? Sorry for, for what?"

"Please understand, sweetheart, I don't want to do this. But I … I have no choice!" His voice was breaking.

Elle was suddenly frantic. What could have happened? "Do what?!"

"I'm sorry, but … Elnora Barstow, you're under arrest …"

THIRTEEN

"What?" Elle screeched. No ... this was her worst nightmare coming true. Her knees went weak and for a brief moment she thought she might topple over, but she didn't. She just stood and stared at Spencer in shock.

The townsfolk began to murmur. The Davis family sat with the same shocked look as everyone else, except for Nellie, who had a smirk on her face.

"What's this all about?" Clayton snapped. "Give me that note." He held out his hand, and Spencer gave it to him. Clayton read the brief missive and lowered it. "Good God. A U.S. Marshal ... coming here?" he said, then turned to Elle. "For you."

Elle shook her head, speechless. A U.S. Marshal? What did that mean? Oh good Lord, it couldn't be!

Spencer grabbed her hand and pulled her away from the altar. "We have to take care of this. Now."

"But Spencer!" the preacher called after him. "What about your wedding?"

"It'll have to wait!" he called over his shoulder as he yanked Elle along behind him, Clayton and Tom following closely.

"Oh, this can't be happening!" Mrs. Riley cried.

Mrs. Davis suddenly stood. "Well, I am certainly not going to sit here and wait for a wedding that will never be!"

Mrs. Riley turned to her. "It most certainly will, Nellie Davis! Just as soon as my boys discover what all this is about!"

"Sit down, Nellie," Mr. Davis urged.

To no avail. "It's quite obvious what it's about!" Mrs. Davis shot back. "Spencer's *mail-order bride* is in some sort of trouble with the law! I might have known!"

Gasps rose up throughout the sanctuary. People stood and looked after the four that just left, and some of the men ran out of the church after them.

"Calm down, all of you! It's not what you think!" Mrs. Riley called over the din of voices, gasps and mumbled accusations.

"Come along, Charlotte!" Mrs. Davis huffed as she exited the pew. "No need to stay any longer for this charade!"

Charlotte sat and watched as her mother made her way down the aisle, then turned to her father.

Mr. Davis looked at her, took out a handkerchief and dabbed at his forehead. "Go with your mother, Charlotte. If for nothing else than to keep her from embarrassing me further," he added darkly.

Charlotte slowly nodded, then left the pew to chase after her mother.

Abbey turned to Billy. "Don't just stand there, Billy, *do* something!"

Billy looked out over the church. At this point all the townspeople were standing, their voices growing louder by the minute.

BANG!

Perhaps putting a round from his revolver into the church's ceiling wasn't the best idea, but he had to admit that it concentrated everyone's attention wonderfully. He grinned sheepishly at the preacher before he spoke. "Now calm down, all y'all! There ain't no good reason for ever'body to get worked up. Sheriff Riley'll have this straightened out in no time. Why don't you good folks go on home and we'll letcha know …"

"Dagnabbit!" Widow Rukeyser, who owned the little sawmill outside of town, called from the back. "I wanted to see me a wedding! I done missed Clayton's!" Several others groaned with disappointment as they put on their hats. Weddings didn't happen very often in Nowhere, so they were kind of a big deal.

Billy watched as folks grumbled and stood. He took in the church, the ribbons, the eager crowd and … Abbey. "Wait!"

The townsfolk turned to him.

"You want a wedding? I'll give you a wedding!"

A low-pitched squawk came from the middle of the church. "What!" Mr. Davis, who had been the only person still sitting, popped up from his seat. "What are you saying, son?"

"I think ya know, sir," Billy said as he reached his hand out to Abbey. She took it, and he went down on one knee. "Abbey Davis, I love you madly, an' I don't know if I can wait through months more o' courtin'! Will you marry me?"

Abbey let loose a high-pitched squeal to match her father's. "Yes! Yes, yes, yes!"

Mr. Davis gasped, dropped back into the pew and wiped his forehead with his handkerchief once more. "This is all so sudden ..."

"Oh, go ahead, Hiram!" Mr. Quinn, sitting in the pew in front of him, urged. "Let the younguns get hitched! Then you'll only have Charlotte to marry off."

Mr. Davis stopped his dabbing, his brow raised at the idea.

"It'll save you a passel of money too – the church is already set up," Mrs. Quinn turned around and added.

Mr. Davis looked at her. "You have a point. And Billy's a good boy – I know he'll take care of her properly."

"What's a couple of months?" Mr. Quinn chimed in. "They're gonna marry anyway, everyone in town knows it."

"And besides," Mr. Davis said with a conspiratorial grin. "Nellie's been giving me grief about Billy – but for once, she isn't here to interfere …"

The Quinns said nothing, only chuckled.

Abbey, having been too lost in Billy's eyes to hear the conversation, turned to her father.

"Please, Daddy?" she pleaded.

Slowly Mr. Davis stood up from the pew. "Billy?"

Billy gulped, got up off his knee and stood straight. "Yessir?"

"You gonna take good care of my daughter?"

"Yessir!"

"And you're gonna bring her back to visit her old pa on occasion?"

Billy and Abbey stared at each other, stunned. How did he know they had planned on leaving town?

"Oh, come on, kids! I love my wife, and my eldest daughter too, but I know they're a trial. I didn't figure you'd want to stay too close – I just don't want you to go too far either!"

Billy blinked a few times, then responded, "That's … that's fine with us, sir."

"Then it's settled!" Mr. Davis stepped out of the pew and looked over the rest of the congregation. "Don't nobody go anywhere! We're gonna have ourselves a wedding!"

The townspeople cheered in excitement, and quickly retook their seats as Billy led Abbey before the preacher.

The preacher glanced up at the hole in the ceiling then at Billy. "This is highly irregular…"

"Oh my goodness!" Mrs. Riley cried. "What about Spencer and Elle?"

Billy leaned toward her. "If I know Spencer, he'll have this fixed quick-like. Go fetch 'em and bring 'em back here. By the time the preacher's done with us, he can marry them! It's worth a try."

"Wait!" Abbey called. "My dress!"

"Dress?" Mr. Davis asked, then slapped his forehead. "That's right, your dress!"

She turned to Billy. "I already have a wedding dress made! It won't take long to fetch. Oh please, Billy, if we're going to be married, I want to be able to wear my dress!"

Summer, who'd been standing off to one side in shocked silence, finally snapped out of it. She turned to Mrs. Riley. "Why don't you take the wagon to the Davises' and get Abbey's dress? Drop me off at the sheriff's office on the way." Then, to the townsfolk: "We'll have not one wedding, but two! In the meantime, why doesn't everyone go to Hank's and have lunch! We'll be back here in less than two hours!"

"Summer, are you sure about this?" Mrs. Riley asked.

"Trust me, it'll all work out fine."

"Oh, dear Lord, I hope you're right!"

"So do I," Summer whispered under her breath, thinking of Elle.

"A U.S. Marshal? But how did a U.S. Marshal know about any of this?" Elle cried as she paced about the jail in her wedding dress.

"Calm down, sweetie, we'll get this sorted out," Spencer assured her as he took one of her hands and pulled her into his arms.

"You know, she's supposed to be behind bars," Clayton mused.

Spencer glared at his brother. "I am *not* putting my bride in a jail cell and you know it!"

"I wouldn't either. But you're going to have to come up with a good reason why a woman wanted for two murders isn't behind bars when that marshal gets here."

Elle did her best to stifle a sob. How had it come to *this*? She'd worried about the man she'd shot, but never thought that she'd be blamed for killing Jethro! What upset her the most was the knowledge that Jethro was no more. He'd given his life to save her, to make sure she got to the train station and safely away from New Orleans and the evil men in it.

Unable to help herself any longer, she buried her face in her hands and wept.

Spencer held her tighter. "Shhh, we'll get this straightened out. I just need a moment to think."

"What is there to think about?" Elle said through her tears. "An innocent man is dead. He didn't do anything but help me!"

"I'm sorry he's gone, sugar. I know you're grieving over his death, but we've got to keep our heads. Can you think of anything else that happened that day? Anything you haven't told us that we can use in your defense when the marshal gets here?"

"Nothing, I … I've told you everything … Oh, Spencer!"

Clayton had begun to pace the office when Summer burst in. "Clayton!"

He went straight to her and took her in his arms. "Where's Ma?"

"She's with the Quinns. They're headed over to the Davises' to get Abbey's wedding dress."

"What?!" both Riley men said.

"Abbey and Billy are getting married *now*?" Elle said as she sniffed back her tears. "Well, no sense letting the church go to waste, I suppose." She looked up at Spencer, sniffled again, then buried her face in his chest.

He held her close, kissed the top of her head, then looked at Clayton. "Billy's resourceful, I'll give him that."

"Yes, but I think he's also stalling for time," Summer said. "He knows it will look better if you fix this quickly and marry today."

"Spencer, she's right," Elle said as she looked up at him. "I didn't want anything like this to happen! It's one of the reasons I thought I couldn't marry you. I didn't want anything marring your reputation as sheriff!"

He smiled down at her. "My reputation isn't as important to me as you are. I will not have the first arrest I make as sheriff be that of my future bride." He sighed. "Maybe I should have ignored that note and gone on with the wedding." She smiled through her tears and held him tight, and he kissed her.

"Except that your deputy came crashing in, in front of half the town, and made it look like something you needed to take care of right away," Clayton said. "Anyway, you did the right thing. And we *will* get this taken care of."

"Which is why I ran on ahead!" Summer interjected. "I got to thinking, how could a U.S. Marshal know of this so quickly?"

"'Cause a U.S. Mahshal can."

All heads turned to the man standing in the doorway of the sheriff's office.

He stepped into the room and glared at them. "Hello – ah'm Mahshal Jim Phebus. And you, young lady," he said as he closed the distance between himself and Elle, "are undah arrest."

And Elle froze. Because while it didn't seem like Spencer or Clayton recognized the man's accent, she did, and was pretty sure Summer did as well. Jim Phebus' drawl was as thick as mud – Louisiana bayou mud.

Marshal Phebus grabbed Elle's arm and tried to pull her out of Spencer's embrace.

Spencer took her other arm and pulled back. "Take your hands off of her!"

The marshal glared at Spencer. "Now, you ain't dumb enough to ahgue with a United States Mahshal, are you, son?"

Spencer studied the man. He was as tall as Spencer but thin, his hair graying at the temples. His eyes were also a dull gray, and he had a hooked nose and thin lips. He looked more criminal than lawman. "What's this all about?"

"You got mah telegraph message, Ah take it?"

"Yes, only moments ago," Spencer said, trying to keep from exploding at the man.

"Then whah ain't this woman in a jail cell?"

"Because we were about to get married!"

Phebus looked at Elle in her wedding dress. "So Ah see."

"How can you not?" Clayton said dryly.

"And I'd like to see your badge," Spencer demanded.

Marshal Phebus sighed and rolled his eyes, then shrugged before he unbuttoned his coat, pulled the left lapel aside and showed both men the badge he wore underneath.

Elle felt Spencer's body stiffen at the sight. He closed his eyes and took a deep breath. When he opened his eyes again, he said, "I'm sorry, honey. But I have no choice."

"Now that's maw like it," Phebus said. "Well, Sheriff, looks like Ah just saved you from marryin' a muhderess." He let go of Elle's arm.

Spencer once again pulled her against him and hugged her. "I promise to get this straightened out. You'll be free by suppertime."

"Free?" Elle gasped. "Does this mean…"

"Lock her up, Sheriff, or Ah'll see you removed from yaw office," Marshal Phebus ordered.

Spencer sighed in resignation and let Elle go. He opened a drawer in the nearby desk and pulled out a ring of keys.

"Oh Elle," Summer began, but Elle raised a hand to her friend to quiet her. She squared her shoulders and looked straight ahead as Spencer guided her toward the cell area. The marshal watched him, one hand on his gun.

He reluctantly opened a cell door and motioned for Elle to enter. "I'm sorry, sugar. I'll fix this, I promise."

Elle looked at him. "I love you," she whispered.

Spencer smiled back. "I know you do. I love you, too."

She smiled and, doing her best to suppress a sob, walked into the jail cell.

"Ah'll make this shawt and sweet," Marshal Phebus declared. "Won't take long, Ah promise. You just sign the necessary papehs and Ah'll be on mah way."

"On your way? You just got here!" Clayton said as he let Summer go and took a threatening step toward the marshal.

"Don't get uppity with me, boy – Ah'm heah on official business. This woman muhdered two men back in N'awlins, and Ah aim to take her back to hang."

"Hang?!" Everyone in the room (not to mention a few extra just entering it) cried in shock.

Nellie Davis went straight to Clayton. "What's the meaning of this? Who's going to hang?"

"Now don't be like the lady who fell off the wagon," Marshal Phebus warned. "Get on outta heah!"

Mrs. Davis narrowed her eyes. "Well, I never!"

Phebus turned back to Spencer. "Where can Ah get some vittles? Ah'd like somethin' before Ah head on out with mah prisoner."

"You just got here!" Spencer repeated.

"No sense wasting time. Ah need to start

back – soonah the bettah, as fah as Ah'm concehned."

"Where did you say you were from?" Summer asked.

He looked at her, through her, and licked his lips. "Ah didn't. What's it to ya?"

Mrs. Davis again narrowed her eyes at him. Charlotte stood behind her, looking like she was about to faint.

"I'm going to the telegraph office!" Clayton said.

Spencer still stood next to the cell, holding Elle's hands through the bars. "Who on earth are you sending a message to?"

"Uncle Harlan. Who else?"

Spencer smiled. If anyone could help them straighten out this mess quickly, it was their uncle, the sheriff of Clear Creek. He was older, and he knew about every marshal in the Northwest. Next to playing checkers, Uncle Harlan loved law trivia.

"Now who's this Uncle Hahlan?" Marshal Phebus drawled.

"Never mind, Hank's restaurant is just down the street," Spencer said. "You can get something to eat there."

Phebus smiled. "Don't mind if Ah do. But Ah can't leave a prisonah." He looked over his shoulder at the Davis women, specifically Charlotte. "Be a good miss an' go fetch me somethin'," he said as he reached into a pocket, pulled out a coin and tossed it to her. "A sandwich'll do nicely."

Mrs. Davis raised her chin in indignation.

"My daughter is not some pickaninny to be ordered about!"

The marshal looked Charlotte up and down. "No, Ah should say not."

Mrs. Davis's mouth dropped open in shock. "Well! Come along, Charlotte – this oaf can get his own food!" She grabbed her daughter by the arm and stormed out of the sheriff's office. Clayton took Summer's hand and quickly followed, leaving Spencer standing there, his face set in firm resolve. Marshal Phebus glared determinedly back.

But Spencer had made up his mind. The only way that marshal was going to take Elle out of Nowhere was over his dead body.

FOURTEEN

"Clayton, there's something funny going on with that marshal," Summer said as he pulled her along beside him. "Nothing about this seems right."

"That's not all that isn't right!" Mrs. Davis spat as she turned to them and put one hand on her hip. "That man speaks very poorly for a Southern gentleman!"

"What are you talking about?" Clayton asked, his brow furrowed in frustration.

"I grew up in Mississippi, and let me tell you, no Southern gentleman would have such abhorrent manners or bad speech. In fact, you can tell where he's from by the way he talks!"

"So can I," Summer affirmed.

Clayton didn't trust Nellie Davis' judgment, but he certainly trusted his wife's. "What are you saying?"

"You're from the North, Clayton – to you all Southern accents probably sound alike. But natives can tell the difference. That man's from the Louisiana bayou … not from New Orleans, but from someplace nearby."

"And 'being like the lady who fell off the wagon'," Nellie chimed in, "it means 'keep your nose out of my business.' But that's a country expression, and a low one to boot! No gentleman would speak to a lady like that, and certainly not a lawman!"

Clayton looked from one woman to the other, trying to get his head around this. "Are you saying you don't think he's an actual marshal?"

"I'm saying that *something* about that Jim Phebus is suspicious," Summer answered, and Nellie nodded her head in agreement.

Clayton's mind was made up – if Summer and Nellie Davis were actually *agreeing* on something, it had to be an unquestionable fact. "All right. I need to get that message off to Uncle Harlan quickly then, and see if he can confirm our suspicions."

"Clayton?" Charlotte begged. "How can we help?"

Clayton and Summer both stared at her. Was she serious? Mrs. Davis was helping them, but only as a by-product of her complaining, not to solve the mystery. Charlotte was acting like she genuinely wanted to help.

Of course, she'd acted that way before …

Clayton had to act fast, though – there wasn't time for a lot of deliberation on Charlotte's motives. "Okay, Charlotte – go back to the jail and stay with Spencer and Elle until we get back from the telegraph office. We've got to stall that marshal – if he is one – for as long as possible."

"Charlotte, you will do no such thing!" Mrs. Davis said in shock. "I want you to march right back to that church and tell your father we're going home! We don't need to get mixed up in this any more than we already are!"

"But Mother," Charlotte pled. "Can't you see how serious this is? Do you really want that man back there to haul Miss Barstow off so he can hang her?"

Mrs. Davis's jaw tightened as she sucked in a breath through her nose. "Charlotte Varina Davis, you get back to the church this instant!"

"What if it were me or Abbey in the same predicament?"

"It is *not* you or Abbey, is it? I will not have you wrapped up with some cold-blooded killer!"

"But Elle Barstow is no more a cold-blooded killer than you are a, a … a soiled dove!"

Mrs. Davis's face turned white. "I will deal with you at home, young lady," she hissed, then spun on her heel and stomped back the way she'd come, passing Mrs. Riley and the Quinns as she did.

"Oh dear, what's happening?" Mrs. Riley said. "We stopped at the sheriff's office, but Spencer said to meet you at the telegraph office! Who is that awful man with Spencer? And where's Elle?"

"Elle is in a jail cell, Ma." Clayton told her.

She and Mrs. Quinn gasped.

"That other man claims he's a U.S. Marshal, sent for Elle's arrest, but we have our doubts. I'm going to wire Uncle Harlan and sees what he says. We need to keep that man here until we find out for sure."

"But Clayton … what if he's not a real

marshal?" Ma Riley asked.

Clayton raised an eyebrow and smiled. "Well, then Spencer will finally be able to make his first arrest."

Elle paced back and forth in her cell as Spencer leaned against the bars. "You're a beautiful bride," he suddenly said.

She stopped and looked at him. His face was steady, his emotions calm. He'd been like a rock ever since his mother and the others left. In fact, as far as she knew, they didn't even know she'd been locked up. "You look pretty handsome yourself ..."

"Stop that talkin'!" Marshal Phebus yelled. "Sheriff, leave the prisonah alone an' get on outta heah!"

Elle watched as Spencer's jaw clenched. "I'll be close by," he whispered to her.

She smiled and nodded as she watched him go up the short hall to the office. The marshal went to the door of the cell area, glared at her, then slammed it shut.

She sat on the cot in the cell and wrapped the one blanket it had around her to keep the chill away. What a wedding day this was turning out to be! Here she was, alone in a cold jail cell, facing two charges of murder. She supposed there were worse situations, but at the moment couldn't think of one.

She sat there what seemed a good long while

and stared at the floor as she listened for anything that might be happening up front. Unfortunately, she could hear nothing. What was she to do? *Oh Lord, if ever there was a time I needed Your help, it's now!*

The door to the cell area suddenly opened, pulling her from her prayer. Charlotte Davis stepped through the door, a basket in her hand.

Elle frowned at the ceiling and mumbled, "I asked for help, Lord …."

"I brought you something to eat. You must be half starved by now," Charlotte said.

The marshal once again slammed the door, making Charlotte jump. She yelped, then quickly made her way to the cell. "Mother's right, that's a very rude man." She pulled a linen napkin back to reveal several sandwiches. "Here, have one. Hank made them."

Elle got up from the cot and went to the bars. She could hardly think of food at a time like this … but eating didn't require thinking, and she hadn't eaten since breakfast. She reached through the bars and took a sandwich.

Charlotte glanced at the door behind her. "Clayton suspects that this marshal isn't who he says he is. He sent me to keep you and Spencer company while he and Summer find out."

"So where are Clayton and Summer?" Elle asked, alarmed. She wanted Clayton back here. Frankly, she wanted as many bodies between her and Jim Phebus as possible – Clayton, Summer, Ma Riley, the entire Grand Army of the Republic if it could be procured.

"They were headed over to the telegraph

THE NEW YEAR'S BRIDE

office, so they could send a message to Clayton's Uncle Harlan – he's the sheriff down in Clear Creek. Clayton says he knows every marshal in these parts and then some. If he's from somewhere nearby, their uncle will have heard of him."

"Nearby? But this man's clearly from ..." Then it hit her. "Of course! No one from Louisiana could have come after me that fast! No one there knew where I was going – except Mrs. Ridgley, of course."

"Who is Mrs. Ridgley?" asked Charlotte.

"She runs the Ridgley Mail-Order Bride Service. Well, I suppose Jethro knew where I was going too, but Jethro's ..." Elle turned away, unable to speak.

"I don't believe you did anything," Charlotte blurted stubbornly. "It's not in you."

Elle spun on her. "How would you know? You don't know me, Charlotte. No one here does. How long before Spencer and his family begin to doubt me?" She said the last part more to herself than to Charlotte.

"I don't know you, but I know me." Charlotte paused before continuing "Someone like me doesn't treat others with the kindness you've shown without expecting to get nothing out of it."

Elle's brow furrowed. "What do you mean?"

"Take it from someone who always has a motive behind what she does. That's what I learned from my mother – always see what you can get out of it. But you ... you could have let me walk home from the mercantile that day and freeze half to death, but you didn't. Maybe I even deserved it, for some of the things I've said and done to Summer … and to you." Charlotte sighed and hung her head. "But I would never wish any real harm to come to either of you. Not like that man out there. I don't trust him and neither does Clayton."

A tear came to Elle's eye. "Thank you, Charlotte. That means a lot to me."

Charlotte was suddenly nervous after her confession. "Well, you'd better eat something. Who knows how long we'll be in here –"

The door suddenly swung open and Marshal Phebus stepped into the hall. "Not long at all, my deahs. Not long at all."

Clayton and Summer were focused on Albert Stephens, the telegraph operator. They'd found him at Hank's having a late lunch, along with quite a few of Nowhere's residents as they waited for the wedding – whichever wedding it was – that would get underway in the next hour.

Mr. Stephens finally finished sending the message and looked up at them. "That does it. One message to Clear Creek, another to New Orleans. Hope this helps. Is there anything else I can do for you, Sheriff?"

"No, Albert. You've been very helpful – thank you. Now all we can do is wait for a reply."

"Well, it being Sunday, I ain't sure if Clear

Creek's telegraph office is even open. Most
small towns have their offices closed today.
New Orleans is another matter – I'm sure
they're open."

"You did mark the message urgent, right?"
Clayton asked.

"Yes sir, I did."

"Good," Summer replied. "Now all we have
to worry about is keeping that marshal busy
until we hear from either Uncle Harlan or Mrs.
Ridgley. Surely she must know what's going
on!"

"I'm sure she does as it was her man that …"
Clayton suddenly stopped. "Wait a minute.
Didn't Elle tell us that Mrs. Ridgley's man was
alive when she left him, and that she didn't
know if the man she'd shot was dead?"

"Yes, why?" Summer asked.

"Think about it. Elle said she heard men
coming, and that Mrs. Ridgley's man Jethro told
her to run. Those men never saw her. If you
were Jethro, would you tell them anything if
you thought they wished her harm?"

"Of course not," Summer said, then caught
on. "But the other man, the one she shot, was in
no shape to say anything – not even if he was
still alive! So if Jethro is supposed to be dead,
how would they know where to find Elle? How
could they discover where Mrs. Ridgley sent
her?"

"Unless they already knew," Clayton
finished for her.

Summer scowled. "I doubt that Jim Phebus is
a marshal at all."

"Which would explain why he's in such an all-fired hurry to get out of here. Where do you suppose he got his hands on a U.S. Marshal's badge?" Clayton stopped, and paled. "When did Red Ned and that other fella – Sam Cooke, that was his name – when did Marshal Leigh haul them out of here?"

"New Year's Day. I remember – I wanted you at home for when Spencer's bride arrived, but you didn't have the time because Marshal Leigh was coming to ..." Summer trailed off and looked at Clayton in shock. "Oh, no. You don't think…"

"It's exactly what I think. This Phebus, or whatever his name really is, could've ambushed Marshal Leigh, taken his badge and showed up here to take Elle. But who would want her so badly? That's the part I don't understand."

"I think I do." Summer walked over to the pot-bellied stove to warm up. "Remember what Elle said about Mr. Slade? If anyone's behind this, he is."

Clayton joined her at the stove. "What makes you say that?"

"Because I saw him. I saw how mad he got when Mrs. Ridgley refused to let him know anything about me. He wanted me for his … *business*. She protected me and got me out of New Orleans as fast as she could. But I still remember how angry he was when Mrs. Ridgley refused to cooperate with him."

"That does it!" Clayton said as he spun on his heel. "Elle's not spending one more minute in that cell! I don't care who that man is, I'm having Spencer lock him up!"

Summer nodded. "I'll head on over to the mercantile and tell Ma and the Quinns."

"Sweetheart, be careful. If he's one of this Mr. Slade's men, then he may be as dangerous to you as he is to Elle."

"You're right. I will be careful." She pulled him close and gave him a good hard kiss. "Let's go."

They stormed out of the telegraph office. Summer turned off at the mercantile, while Clayton continued down the boardwalk to confront this so-called Marshal Phebus, determined to settle the matter as soon as possible. He wasn't about to let anyone, let alone some phony marshal, delay his brother's wedding any longer!

"You're not a real marshal, are you," Elle stated rather than asked as Phebus pulled both her and Charlotte away from the cell and toward the main sheriff's office.

"Why, whatevah gave you that idea?" he drawled.

"You're hurting my arm," Charlotte complained.

"Dahlin', Ah'll huht a lot moah 'n that if ya don't hush now."

"She has nothing to do with this – let her go," Elle demanded.

"Ah don't see as yaw in any position to give

me ordehs," Phebus said with a smile as they reached the office. "Last one to trah and ordeh me around – lookit what happened." He indicated with his head to his left.

Elle looked – and screamed.

Spencer, her husband-to-be, her protector, the town sheriff and the man she loved … Spencer was tied to a chair, unconscious. His head lolled to one side, and there was a bruise forming at the base of his skull. Phebus must've hit him from behind.

"HUSH!" Phebus barked at her. "Hush, or Ah'll do wuhse to you!"

Frightened, Elle managed to bring her noise down to a series of whimpers.

"Now that's bettah. Come along quiet-like, both o' ya, an' everyone'll be bettah off."

"Why are you taking her?" Elle asked of Charlotte. "What has she done?"

Phebus looked at Charlotte and grinned like the Cheshire cat. "She ain't done nothin' – leastwise, not yet. But Ah'm lookin' foahwahd to findin' out what she *can* do." He turned back to Elle. "Yaw the prize, though. She's just a bonus."

"Who sent you? If it's Mr. Slade, you'll never get us all the way back to New Orleans! Spencer and his brother will hunt you down and …"

"Do I hafta put a gag on ya to get some peace?!" Phebus yelled in her face.

Elle, eyes wide, said nothing more.

Phebus nodded, as if to say *that's moah lahk it*, and dragged both women out to a prison wagon. He lifted Elle up, chained her hands behind her to a large metal ring bolted to the sturdy wagon bed, then did the same with Charlotte, who looked like she was in shock. Once done with that, he got out a couple pieces of cloth. "Just faw safety's sake, Ah think Ah'd best gag ya anyways. Nevah know who maht be listenin'."

Elle watched him bind Charlotte's mouth. "You'll still never get to New Orlmmmph!"

Phebus gagged her before she could finish. "Silly chickie – we ain't goin' to N'Awlins. We only goin' ... naw, nevah ya mind wheah we goin'. Suufahce to say, I have me an establishment o' mah own, an' you'll both make fahne additions to it." He tightened the knot and stepped back to admire his handiwork. "An' if you must know, it was mah brothah that infawmed me o' you. He wuhks faw Slade, but he ain't as stupid. Slade wanted me to kill ya, can you believe that? But ya know the ol' sayin' – waste not, want not." He grinned evilly again.

Elle wanted to give him what for – actually, she wanted to grab his gun and see if she couldn't go two-for-two – but her hands were shackled, and her words were cut off.

He saw the frustration on her face and chuckled. "Ohhhh, y'all got some spirit, Ah see. Ah think Ah'll enjoy breakin' that spirit once we get wheah we goin'. Mah brothah said you weah a beauty, and he was raht." He backed out of the wagon, shut the door and locked it.

Elle listened and cringed as she heard him climb up onto the wagon seat and slap the horses with the reins. She felt the wagon lurch forward and looked at Charlotte, who sat silently, her own eyes filling with tears. Good God, what was happening? Did Slade really want her killed? And what about all this talk of being a fine addition to the man's establishment? Who *was* this man?

Elle's eyes suddenly widened. Phebus, or whatever his real name was, looked familiar. Elle was sure she'd seen him before. But where? *Think – think of the people in New Orleans ...*

She pulled on the chain, to no avail. The prison wagon was like a cell on wheels, built to keep strong men from escaping. How much chance did two helpless women stand? Spencer was knocked out and tied up in the sheriff's office. Clayton was at the telegraph office, waiting for word from Clear Creek. How long would it be before they discovered Phebus had taken off with them?

The wagon continued to roll along at a fast pace. How long had they been gone already? It couldn't be long – five, ten minutes – but every second gave their kidnapper an advantage.

Lord, I know I asked for help earlier, but right now would be a real good time to send some! You may not have another chance –

A shot rang out, then another. Elle could hear Phebus cursing up a storm over the sound of the horses' thundering hooves. Spencer and Clayton! They'd come for her! It had to be them!

Another shot, this one louder. Phebus was firing back.

There was a sudden commotion outside the wagon. There was a barred window in the side, but chained as she was, Elle couldn't stand up to peek out of it.

More shots were fired, many of them from Phebus' gun from the sound of it. Elle cringed when she heard a muffled grunt, then shouts from far away, but how could she tell what had happened? The wagon was still barreling along, and the noise from the galloping horses and rattling wheels was loud. For all she knew, the men chasing after them were extremely close. She certainly hoped and prayed they were!

Another shout came. This time it was someone yelling "Whoa!" several times at the horses, possibly a lone rider coming up alongside the wagon. She felt her heart leap into her chest as the wagon slowed, then finally stopped.

She heard another horse gallop up, and a rider clumsily dismount. Whoever he was fumbled with the lock. "Elle?"

Spencer! But Elle couldn't cry out, nor could Charlotte, gagged as they were.

More riders could be heard coming toward the wagon. Another shot, this time breaking the lock on the prison wagon.

Then Spencer swung the door open. "Elle!" He clambered up into the wagon, went straight to her and pulled the gag out of her mouth. "Elle, are you all right?" He pulled her into his arms as best he could, and immediately saw her shackled wrists chained to the ring in the floor. "Oh boy … this could be a problem …"

"Spencer!" Elle interrupted. "Charlotte …"

"Charlotte?" Spencer turned and gasped. He'd been so eager to rescue Elle, he hadn't even noticed Charlotte was there. That whack on the back of his head must've rattled his brains but good! "Good grief! Charlotte, I'm sorry!"

"Mmmmmph!" Charlotte replied as she glared at him.

"Right!" he agreed. He crawled over to where she sat in the corner and removed her gag.

"Oh, that's better!" she groaned. "Didn't you even notice I was gone?"

"I apologize, Miss Davis, but that Jim Phebus knocked me out just after you arrived at my office, and … well, I'm not quite all the way back yet," he finished with an embarrassed chuckle.

"Well … all right, but can you unchain me?"

"Sure can … as soon as we find where Phebus hid the keys. And he's …" He waved his hand vaguely in the direction they'd come. "… somewhere back there."

"Did you shoot him?" Elle asked, half hoping he had.

"Well, Deputy Turner shot him, to be precise. He has the fastest horse I've ever seen, and a pretty fast draw to boot. I think he went back to check him for identification."

"You think?!" Charlotte asked pointedly.

Spencer had no time for this act. His voice was low, but firm. "With all respect, ma'am, let's see how well you operate after getting knocked cold, then riding a horse top-speed a few miles."

Charlotte nodded and said no more.

Just then Clayton rode up, holding a small ring of keys in one hand. "You need these, Spence?"

"Sure do!" Spencer called back. Clayton tossed him the key ring, and he immediately unlocked the shackles on Elle's wrists, then Charlotte's. Charlotte actually looked at him gratefully. Hmmm … what had happened while he was out cold that would make Charlotte act … well, a little nicer?

But that was a mystery he could solve another time – right now, he had other things on his mind. Spencer turned from Charlotte and pulled Elle into his arms. "Elle, are you sure you're all right?"

"I'm fine now – are you sure *you're* all right?" Gingerly, she reached over and touched the growing lump on the back of his head.

Spencer winced. "Yeah, I'll live. I gotta pretty hard head, you know."

"Isn't that the truth?" Clayton muttered under his breath, and Charlotte stifled a giggle.

"Who was that man?" Elle asked.

"Not who he claimed to be, that's for sure. Clayton and I will get to the bottom of that, don't you worry. You've got more important things to think about."

Elle looked up at him, reveling in the safety of his arms. "Like what?"

"Like getting married – if you're still up to it. There's a church full of people back there waiting for us. Billy and Abbey are probably taking their vows right now."

She looked into his eyes and felt like she could fall into them and never come out – or want to. "I can't think of anything I'd like more." She pulled him close. "Marry me, Spencer Riley. Marry me right now."

He smiled and pulled her into his arms. "I will." He kissed her soundly, then helped her out of the wagon.

Clayton offered a hand to Charlotte to help her out. "Well, I guess it's time we got back. You're all right, I take it – he didn't hurt you?"

Charlotte blew a loose curl out of her face. "The only thing hurt right now is my pride. If only I had a handsome man come hightail it after me to see to *my* rescue. But … well, I guess I'll just have to wait my turn." She stared at her shoe. "Besides, I suppose my pride could use a good beating …"

Clayton raised an eyebrow, pleasantly surprised. This wasn't the Charlotte Davis he knew … it was an improvement. Whatever had changed, he hoped it stuck. "Don't worry, Charlotte – one day your prince will come."

"Well he'd better hurry up! I'm not getting any younger, you know!"

Clayton sighed. Back to more-or-less normal, then. "May I escort you to a wedding, then?"

"Along with your wife?"

"Well, of course."

"All right," she responded after a few seconds, smiling weakly and clearly fighting tears. Without another word Clayton tied his horse to the back of the wagon, then helped her up onto the wagon seat.

Spencer helped Elle onto his horse (no small feat given the dress she was wearing), then mounted up behind her. "Remind me never to let you out of my sight once we're married."

Elle smiled at him. She was sitting side-saddle, Spencer's strong arms the only thing holding her in place. "You can't be with me every hour, Spencer. Though I wish you could."

"Who says I can't?"

"You're the sheriff! I'm not the only one around for you to protect, but I'm glad you were around today."

"It's my wedding day, sugar, of course I'm around. But I almost wasn't. If we hadn't figured out Phebus was a phony, I'm not sure we'd have caught up to you as quick as we did."

"It was fast, I'll give you that. Where are we, anyway?"

"Only about three miles out of town. He didn't get far. Tom's hauling his body back to Nowhere."

"He's … dead, then?"

"Yes, honey. He sure is."

She leaned against his chest and rested her head on his shoulder. "Oh, Spencer, I didn't want it to come to this …"

"Hush now, sugar. It wasn't like it was your fault. And you're safe now, both you and Charlotte. We can't ask for much more than that."

"He said he wasn't taking us to New Orleans, that he was taking us someplace else."

"It doesn't much matter now – he won't be going anywhere except a nice deep hole. And to hell, probably."

Spencer held her and whispered words of comfort in her ear all the way back to town – specifically to the church. Once there, he reined in his horse, looked into Elle's eyes, and kissed her firmly.

When he broke the kiss he smiled. "You beat a new scarf any day."

"What?"

His smile broadened. "Ma's made me a new scarf and mittens every Christmas for as long as I can remember. But not this year, this year she gave me you instead. My New Year's bride."

Elle reached up, and stroked his cheek. She should have been cold riding back, but she wasn't. How could she be when her insides were melting? "I love you, Spencer Riley. I was afraid to because of what happened before I came here, but not loving you would have been a bigger crime than anything I did back in New Orleans."

He took her hand in his. "You did nothing but defend yourself and I'll find out what happened. For now…" He raised her hand to his lips and kissed it. "Marry me."

"I will," she said – and gave him a kiss for the ages.

FIFTEEN

Cheers went up throughout the church as Spencer, Elle, Billy and Abbey turned to face the congregation.

"Gentlemen!" the preacher called. "You may kiss your brides!"

They did, and the cheers and whistles became almost deafening. Spencer finally came up for air and smiled at the townspeople of Nowhere. As yet, the people didn't know what had happened, nor the full extent of the danger Elle and Charlotte had been in. Thank the Lord Clayton and Tom had discovered the empty jail cell – and his unconscious state – when they did, or they might have risked losing that scoundrel Phebus' trail.

The timing was perfect in other ways too. No sooner had they re-entered the church, it started to snow like nobody's business. The weather would have made it impossible to track anything, even something the size of a marshal's wagon.

Spencer took Elle's hand and led her to the back of the church amidst more noise and words of congratulations, even an honest-to-goodness rebel yell from Mr. Davis (much to Charlotte's chagrin). He smiled as they reached the church doors and opened them.

Elle gasped with delight. "Oh my! I've never seen anything so beautiful!"

He smiled and held her close, not wanting her to get cold again. "It's not so beautiful when you have to go out and work in it."

"You don't have to go out in this, do you?"

"I do if I want to get you home … Mrs. Riley."

"Oh, Spencer!"

He laughed and kissed her as Clayton and Summer joined them. "Well, little brother, you're married now. How does it feel?"

No answer.

"Spencer … oh." Clayton hadn't realized that his brother was too busy kissing his new wife to answer. Clayton turned to Summer. "Well, you know what they say."

"What?" Summer said with a smile.

"If you can't beat 'em, join 'em." He smiled devilishly, pulled his own wife into his arms and kissed her.

Billy and Abbey watched from right behind them and did the same. The church exploded with clapping, hoots and hollers for the three kissing couples.

One person, however, was silent. Charlotte leaned against the wall and watched the newlyweds, a tear in her eye. She sighed heavily just as someone came to stand beside her.

"Sure is a lot of kissin' goes on in this town,"

Tom Turner observed. "'Course, there's a fair share of it goes on in Clear Creek too."

Charlotte looked at him with a put-upon expression. "And how would you know? Were you doing a lot of kissing back in your home town?"

Tom blushed and glanced at his boots. "No, ma'am, not me. I ain't never had the pleasure."

She stood up straight. As handsome as this man was ... "You've got to be joking."

He looked down at her. "No, ma'am. I am not."

"Really?" she purred.

Tom's eyes widened. "Uh ... it's the honest truth, ma'am."

Charlotte raised an eyebrow and smiled, perhaps a bit too widely. "Well, Mr. Turner, there's a first time for everything ..."

"Er ... I, I think I hear Sheriff Riley calling me! If you'll excuse me, ma'am!" He quickly tipped his hat and fled.

"Oh, fiddle-dee-dee!" Charlotte said, stomping her foot.

"Now, Charlotte, don't despair!" Mrs. Riley said as she came to stand beside her. "One day you'll be married too!"

"Well, I'd sure like to know when *that's* going to happen," she said with a pout. "If this keeps up, I'm going to have to have *my* mother see about getting me a mail-order groom!" Without another word, she walked off.

Mrs. Riley sighed as she watched her go. Then, after making sure no one was looking over her shoulder, she pulled a folded piece of paper and a pencil from her reticule. "Let's see now…," she said to herself as she crossed names off a list. "Clayton … Spencer … Billy – don't have to worry about him now …"

She tapped the pencil against her chin a few times as she looked to the next name: *Matthew Quinn*. "Well, young Dr. Quinn, looks like you're next. And by my calculations, your bride ought to arrive around the same time you do. Won't that be nice?"

"Ma," Spencer called from the church doorway. "What's keeping you?"

Mrs. Riley quickly shoved the paper and pencil back into her reticule. "Oh, nothing! Are you ready to go to Hank's, dear? We thought it best to have the wedding supper there so folks didn't have to drive out to our place in this nasty weather!"

"Ma, you've got that look on your face. You're up to something …"

Mrs. Riley smiled, her eyes bright. "Spencer, I think becoming sheriff has made you far too suspicious."

Spencer shook his head. "Whenever you get *that* look lately, someone ends up married."

"Well, what's wrong with that? Can't I have my sons get married?"

"Yes, but now we *are* married, so there's no need for you to get that look anymore."

Mrs. Riley smiled sweetly. "You're quite right, dear. Shall we go now?"

Spencer eyed her suspiciously before he offered her his arm. His mother took it, and together with his new bride, left the church to attend the wedding supper.

But as they left, Mrs. Riley smiled and winked at Mrs. Quinn. Both knew that Nowhere's next mail-order bride was already on the way.

New Orleans, one week later.

Thaddeus Slade slammed his fist on the table so hard his brandy bottle and glasses rattled and clinked together. "I cannot believe your brother failed me!" he sneered. "Now I've lost two men, and have nothing to show for it! What have you to say for yourself?"

"My brothah was shot doin' what you asked o' him."

"He did *nothing* I asked of him. The girl still lives, as does the other one that managed to escape. And I'm losing money!"

"Maybe ya shouldn't oughta promise goods ya can't delivah."

Slade drew his gun and aimed it at the man sitting on the other side of his desk. "Shut up before I kill you."

The other man didn't flinch, only chuckled. "Ya ain't verah good at that."

"Do you know who you're dealing with?"

"Of cawse. Which is why I ain't a-tall worrehd. But you obviously don't know who yaw dealin' with. Mah employah is lookin' for spee-*cific* goods. Twahce you've failed to delivah. I trust anothah visit to this Mrs. Ridgley should cleah things up? Ya did tell me she had the best eye in the business?"

"Yes, but… she's not very cooperative. Killing the two that got away would have served to make her see reason and come work for me again. Now I'll have to think up some other form of persuasion."

"Think of it fast, Mr. Slade. Mah employah ain't gonna be happy when he fahnds out the only reason you even knew wheah to look was because ya intahcepted a telegraph message from one o' them. Ya got luckeh …and still not luckeh enough." He pulled on a pair of thin leather gloves before he reached for the walking stick leaning against his chair. "We have a shipment to delivah in two months' time, an' ordehs to fill." The man stood, downed what was left of his brandy and stepped to the door. "He wants at least a dozen. You think you can fahnd yaw way to handle that?"

"I'll handle it! Don't think I don't know my business!"

The man smiled. "Be a good man, then, and see to it. Faw once." He left.

Slade drained his own glass and went to the window. He pushed the rich velvet curtains aside and peered down at the street below, and watched the man who'd just paid him a visit get into a fancy black coach. With a flick of the driver's reins, he rode away out of sight.

Slade let the curtain fall back into place. "Well, Mrs. Ridgley," he drawled, "time to pay you another visit. And this time … no niceties."

At the same time in Nowhere …

Elle was jumping up and down, waving the telegraph sheet, tears of joy running down her face. "Jethro's alive! Spencer, isn't it wonderful? They didn't kill him, they didn't!" She launched herself at him and nearly knocked them both onto the bed.

Spencer laughed, took her in his arms and held her. As soon as he'd received the message from the telegraph office, he'd ridden straight home, knowing she'd want to see it. "See? Everything's going to be okay now, monkey. Didn't I tell you Clayton and I would get to the bottom of this?"

"Yes! Yes, you … wait, 'monkey'? I still don't know if I like that …?"

"Well, I think it suits you. Only a monkey could have climbed up onto my horse in a wedding dress like you did."

She smiled at him. "You … are impossible."

"And you are beautiful."

She stood on tiptoe and kissed Spencer full on the mouth, then smiled. "I love you so much."

"I love you too," he laughed. "Enough to nickname you, at any rate."

"Hmmm … maybe I ought to give you a nickname too."

"Like what?" he asked nervously.

Elle smiled mischievously. "Give me some time – I'll think of one."

"That's what I'm afraid of. But I'm so glad everything turned out, and we finally heard from Mrs. Ridgley. I knew that Phebus was a fake." He grimaced. "Too bad about Marshal Leigh, though – he got an even nastier knock on the head than I did, and now we've got two outlaws to recapture."

"I'm glad I was able to remember the man at the train station – I didn't until a few days ago. But they look so much alike, it has to have been Phebus' brother."

Spencer sat down on the bed, and drew Elle down beside him. "It's all coming together now. You shoot a man, no one presses charges, yet Phebus shows up … they all must be in on this. Everything fits." He kissed the top of her head. "Almost everything, anyway. But Clayton and I will find the answers soon enough. In the meantime, what say we start on Ma's Christmas present?"

"Christmas present? Spencer, what on earth are you talking about? It's still January! What could we possibly make for her that would take us until next …"

Spencer grinned.

"Oh, goodness – Spencer!"

"Well? If she gave me a mail-order bride for New Year's Day, can't I give her a grandchild for next Christmas?"

Elle looked at him as his words sunk in … and then a smile of her own grew. "When do we start?"

"How about right now, Mrs. Riley?" He then took her in his arms and saw to it they got his mother's Christmas present well underway.

The End

I hope you enjoyed reading The New Year's Bride, the second book in the Holiday Mail-Order Bride Series. Be sure to check out the rest of the series:

The Christmas Mail-Order Bride (Book One)

His Forever Valentine (Book Three)

Her Irish Surrender (Book Four)

The Springtime Mail-Order Bride (Book Five)

Love in Independence (Book Six)

Love at Harvest Moon (Book Seven)

The Thanksgiving Mail-Order Bride (Book Eight)

The Holiday Mail-Order Bride (Book Nine)

His Mail-Order Valentine (Book Ten)

The Easter Mail-Order Bride (Book Eleven)

A Mid-Summer's Mail-Order Bride (Book Twelve)

And don't forget to have a sneak peek at
HIS FOREVER VALENTINE,
the next installment of this delightful series!

One

New Orleans, January 1871

Eugena Ridgley of The Ridgley Mail-Order Bride Service of New Orleans, Louisiana, had always been a risk-taker, no one ever said otherwise. When she believed in a cause, she believed wholeheartedly. This would explain why her newest client, Sequoia Rose Smith, was being rushed to the train station with a full pillowcase stuffed under her dress. She was alone save for her escort Jethro, who followed at a distance, his keen eyes watching for any sign of trouble. Thankfully, they had been able to elude it. This time.

Sequoia (usually called Rose because, let's face it, Caucasians in that time didn't normally name a child after an Indian) boarded without incident. The conductor, especially gracious once he noted her delicate condition, took her satchel in hand and got her a place to sit.

Several men noticed her lovely dark curls and violet eyes as she passed. But their interest waned when they spotted her mid-section, and they all turned away and searched for something else to study. Even dust motes floating in the sun's rays would do. A pregnant woman traveling alone meant trouble, no matter how pretty she was. And in the middle of Reconstruction, with the Civil War fresh in everyone's mind, a corrupt administration in Washington and outlaws and Indians on the warpath in the West, there was enough trouble to go around without looking for more.

Catching their sudden disinterest, Rose smiled. Mrs. Ridgley was right – men *did* steer clear of her when she appeared to be in a family way. Of course, the only thing Rose was expecting (aside from what was stuffed under her dress) was to catch the train without incident. So far, so good.

One problem remained with the ruse: how, and more importantly *when*, was she going to remove the bundle of petticoats from beneath her clothing? She'd hoped to put them back in her satchel before she boarded, but she'd arrived late and had to jump on the train immediately. Now she had the disapproving eyes of the other passengers on her.

Well, she'd just have to worry about that later. For now, she sighed in relief as the whistle blew and the conductor called out his last "all aboard!"

She'd done it! Rose was free from her life at Winslow's Orphanage and on her way to the town of Nowhere up in the Washington Territory to be a mail-order bride! She was the third girl Mrs. Teeters had sent to the Northwest this way, and she couldn't be happier. She'd liked living at Winslow, mind – as much as one could like the life of an orphan – and wouldn't have minded staying. But they had an inconvenient rule: once you reached your eighteenth birthday, you were on your own

And in New Orleans, still recovering from the war, the prospects for an eighteen-year-old girl with no family and no job experience other than taking care of fellow orphans were limited and unattractive. Unscrupulous men frequented the city sections containing the orphanages, waiting for young girls gullible or careless enough to be snatched up and put to work in one of their "establishments." And once ensnared, it was almost impossible for the girls to escape …

So needless to say, becoming a mail-order bride not only provided a certain adventure, but according to Mrs. Ridgley was the safest option. Who was she to argue?

There were still dangers to face, of which just getting out of New Orleans had been the first. But she had an adventurous spirit, and going west thrilled her to no end. What would life in the tiny northwestern town bring? And what of her future husband, Matthew Quinn? All she knew was that he was a few years older than her, educated in a Northern college, and his family owned the town mercantile. She had her entire journey to think about him and wonder.

Rose settled into her seat, sighed contentedly and smiled in anticipation. As soon as she found an opportunity to lose her burden of petticoats, she would. In the meantime, she planned to enjoy the scenery and dream of a new life full of adventure and romance in the Wild West!

Nowhere, in the Washington Territory …

Matthew Quinn cautiously picked up the bucket of dirty water and carried the sloshing, smelly vessel to the back porch of the mercantile. Once there he lifted the bucket higher (careful, don't spill), turned his face away in disgust, and dumped it out. He closed his eyes at the subsequent splash, and waited before slowly opening one eye. He sighed in relief that he hadn't spilled any on his boots, and turned to the door.

When had he become so fastidious? He'd never been this squeamish before he left for college – he'd studied science and medicine, for Pete's sake, and often had his hands in blood and guts up to his elbows. So why the aversion to some dirty water? He straightened his spectacles, stopped and peered over his shoulder at the puddle in the street.

He shivered, but not from cold. *Germs!*

Ever since he'd read John Snow's articles on the cholera outbreaks of Broad Street in

London, he'd been horrified. The diseases, the fevers, the *deaths,* and worst of all the epidemic proportions! He cringed at the thought and went inside.

He set the bucket down, closed the door and glanced around the kitchen of his family's living quarters in the back of the mercantile. Not much had changed since he'd left for school four years before. His parents had slapped a coat of paint on the place and had the front sign re-done. Different curtains decorated his old room upstairs, and his mother used a new set of china last night at dinner, but other than that, everything was right as he'd left it. Nothing in town seemed to have changed either, and he suspected that if he'd been gone ten years the town would still be the same.

He sighed, walked to the front of the store, and stopped short. *Something* had changed ... His mouth went dry, his knees became like jelly, and his gut twisted into a gigantic knot the likes of which he hadn't felt in years.

She turned around, a vision of loveliness. "Matthew?"

Matthew's spectacles slowly slid down his sweat-covered nose as his brain fogged with mixed emotions. How could he have possibly forgotten this? Four years had passed since he'd seen her, and he was *still* tongue-tied in her presence!

It wasn't until his glasses reached the tip of his nose that he managed to gather his wits and push them back into place. "Hello, Ch-Charlotte."

Charlotte Davis gave him a dazzling smile. "I heard you came back early from school, but I never did understand why." She sashayed her way to the counter, her cream-colored dress making a swishing sound as she approached. He fought against a lovesick sigh as he watched her. "Boston is such a lovely city! Why would you ever leave?"

He swallowed hard. "Be … because," his voice squeaked, "I wanted to come home."

"To *Nowhere*?" she asked with a raised eyebrow. "Why, Matthew Quinn, what did they forget to teach you in that fancy school of yours? You had a chance to get out of this town, and here you are, right back where you started!"

He studied her. She was even more beautiful than he remembered. Her chestnut hair and hazel eyes had him mesmerized. She'd filled out during his four-year absence, the willow-thinness of adolescence blossoming into the woman she'd become. She stood looking at him over the counter, her eyes slowly taking him in, and he wondered what she was thinking.

Clayton Riley … Matthew's shoulders slumped. Of course – what else would she be thinking? Not a day went by when the man's name didn't leave Charlotte's lips.

But hadn't he gotten married recently? Matthew had arrived on the afternoon stage only yesterday. His mother had been so occupied cooking his favorite meal that she hadn't much time to catch him up yet. He thought he'd caught some mention of it that morning, but wasn't paying attention. He was too busy getting fawned over by his mother, and several of her friends, when he went to work. Thankfully, she was preparing lunch, and the matrons who frequented the mercantile in the morning hours had come and gone. Only Charlotte was in the store, alone ... with *him*.

Matthew smiled.

"Has anyone told you what you've missed while you were away?" Charlotte asked.

He shook himself. Was she trying to make conversation? It was usually the other way around. "Um, no, not really. I ... I just got in yesterday ..."

"Oh, well then!" she said as her eyes lit up. "Let me tell you all about it!" She leaned against the counter and stared up at him.

Matthew willed himself not to sweat. It hardly mattered that the January winds howled outside – he'd never been able to remain cool and calm where Charlotte was concerned. "Do tell?"

"Oh yes, *I'll* tell!" she laughed.

His eyes widened at the sound. Good Lord, she had to be the most beautiful woman in the world!

Seeming unaware of her effect on him, she straightened, sighed, and picked at one of her gloves. "Of course you've already heard that Clayton Riley got married ...," she said forlornly.

His heart sank. "No, I hadn't."

She sighed theatrically. "Spencer too – just last week, in fact."

"*Both* the Riley brothers are married?" That

was news. Clayton and Spencer Riley had been the most eligible bachelors in town for years – and now both were out of his way! He again smiled, more broadly this time.

Charlotte noticed and smiled back. "Recently, within a few weeks of each other. Too bad you missed Spencer's wedding. It was kind of a free-for-all. Billy Blake, the deputy, you remember him? Well, he got married the same day."

"He did?" Matthew asked and straightened. Three weddings in Nowhere in the same calendar year was unheard of. But three in less than a month? Inconceivable! "Who did he marry?"

"My sister."

"Abbey?!"

Charlotte looked at the floor, and pulled away from him, her shoulders drooping. "Yes," she whispered sadly. "Quite a bit of marrying has been going on around here of late. Too bad you missed it all."

"Yeah, too bad," he agreed as he gazed into her eyes. A lot could have happened in the last four years. Who knew how many men had come to town and decided to settle? His parents hadn't mentioned the Davises in their letters, largely because they'd never cared for Nellie Davis. But whom else had they mentioned? Drat it all! He couldn't recall.

He swallowed, and before he thought to stop himself asked, "What about you, Charlotte? Are you going to get married?" Maybe it was too abrupt, but he had to find out!

"I'm not sure if I'll ever marry ..."

His head shot up. "What?" he blurted. He'd been so busy trying to remember any mention of new settlers, he wasn't sure he'd heard her right.

She shrugged, and he noticed her eyes glisten. He studied her, his heart hitching at the thought of Charlotte growing old, alone and unwanted. Unfortunately, what things he *had* heard since his arrival involved Charlotte, and none of them good. Maybe he shouldn't have asked after the Davis family last night at dinner – it had gotten him an earful of Charlotte this and Charlotte that and this town would be better off without that Charlotte Davis.

He decided he'd judge for himself. It was hard to believe that someone as adorable as Charlotte could be that evil. Maybe it wasn't as bad as his mother had said ...

She swallowed hard, straightened and forced a smile. Matthew knew it was forced by the way her jaw tightened. He'd made a habit of studying every inch of her face, memorizing it every time he was with her as they'd grown up. He could also see great sadness hidden in the tightness around her mouth, the furrow of her brow.

But where was that great defiance he remembered, as if she was shouting to the world, *no, you'll never break me no matter how hard you try*? It was the trait that seemed to annoy most people, but not Matthew. He thought it a hidden well of strength she drew from when she needed it, each time her heart was broken ...

He'd witnessed Charlotte's heart get broken repeatedly over the years, before he went off to school. Her mother did the most damage, filling the girl's head with ideas of their supposed lost status in the pre-war South, of marrying into the Riley family and having a share in one of the biggest apple farms (if not *the* biggest) in the area. Never mind that the Rileys would've sooner moved to Outer Mongolia than have Thanksgiving dinner with Nellie Davis – Nellie was determined to invade that family, with Charlotte as her weapon of choice.

Nellie Davis's ambition had pounded her daughter's heart with blow after blow, and apparently all for naught – Clayton and Spencer had both chosen someone else, and Charlotte was still unwed, even while her younger sister had gone off and married. Matthew often wondered if Charlotte had really been interested in Clayton, or if she'd just been trapped by her mother's schemes. Who would Charlotte be with if left to her own devices?

And the unaskable question: *could it be me?*

"Are you planning to attend the Valentine's dance?" she asked, pulling him from his thoughts. She walked down the length of the counter, running a gloved finger along the polished wood.

Matthew's eyes gravitated to her small waist as visions of dancing with her in his arms flooded his mind. "I … I hadn't thought about it. Um …"

She turned to him, her face a void. "I see." She reached into her reticule and pulled out a

list. Without looking at him, she walked back
and handed it to him. "Here's what I need." She
slowly raised her eyes, then glanced at the front
windows. "It's nice to have you back,
Matthew," she said softly.

He took the list from her, his heart in a
turmoil. All the fight seemed to have gone out
of her. Where could the spitting, fiery hellion
he'd left back in '66 be hiding? Maybe what his
mother said was true, that Charlotte had become
a prisoner of her own actions, and now, sad and
lonely, she was a far cry from the girl he grew
up with. She'd told him last night what sort of
gossips the Davis women had become, how
conniving and underhanded when it came to
getting what they wanted.

Well, he was familiar with how Mrs. Davis
could be; he'd witnessed her antics all his life.
But Charlotte didn't start to become like her
mother until she got old enough to catch the eye
of the young men in town. At fourteen she
hadn't just been a beauty, but actually quite
sweet, albeit with a habit of speaking out of
turn, and no hesitation to fight for something
she believed in. He'd loved those traits, that
strength. What had happened to quell her
fighting spirit?

Now, it was her melancholy that was
obvious. And Matthew saw something in her
eyes he'd never thought he would. Regret.

"I'll get these things for you, Charlotte," he
said gently. "Wait right here." His heart went
out to her. Then and there he decided to find out
if what his mother had said was true, and

anything else mentioned regarding the Davis family. He needed to find the Charlotte he knew – she had to be in there somewhere!

After all, she was the reason he'd come home.

Charlotte watched as Matthew climbed a stepladder to get a jar off a high shelf. He'd gotten a lot taller since she last saw him. She remembered when they were the same height, and tried not to laugh as she recalled the time she'd punched him in the nose. He didn't cry out – he didn't do anything except stare at her, his fists at his sides, and then walk away.

Abbey told her the next day that he'd been furious, but that he wasn't about to hit a girl. He wouldn't be a man if he did, and besides, his pa would tan his hide if he found out.

She studied him as he busied himself behind the counter to fill her mother's order. His shoulders were broader. His hair had changed from a dirty blonde to golden brown, still thick and with a slight wave. She remembered having her hands in it while playing in the creek down at Mr. Johnson's swimming hole. She'd tried to dunk him after he'd called her a silly name. He dunked her instead, and so she'd taken two fistfuls and pulled him underwater. He in turn had grabbed her ankles and yanked her feet out from under her …

"What are you smiling at, Charlotte?"

Charlotte glanced up. Mrs. Quinn, Matthew's mother, stood on the other side of the counter, eying her cautiously. "Nothing. Just thinking." She approached the counter and stole another glance at Matthew's now-muscular physique. No, he certainly wasn't the gangly boy who went off to Boston four years ago. Matthew Quinn may have left Nowhere a boy, but he'd most definitely come back a man. A very handsome man …

"Have you started on a dress for the Valentine dance, Charlotte?" Mrs. Quinn asked.

"Yes, Abbey and I both have. I'm making my own this year."

"Well, isn't that nice? So how does Abbey like being married?" Mrs. Quinn began to wrap some of Charlotte's purchases in brown paper. Matthew hopped off the ladder and handed her a bottle of hair tonic.

Charlotte found herself staring at his hands. "She's … adjusting. Billy and Daddy get along fine, but …"

Mrs. Quinn leaned forward. "But?"

Charlotte took a deep breath. "Mother … is having a more difficult time of it."

"I see." Mrs. Quinn smirked.

Charlotte caught sight of her curled lip and turned away.

Matthew swallowed hard. He decided (as he searched for another bottle of Professor Pomodori's Hair Tonic) to ask Charlotte to the Valentine's dance. From the sounds of it, no one else would escort her, which gave him the perfect opportunity. "Er, Charlotte?"

She turned to him, her face softened. "Yes?"

"I was wondering … if you don't happen to have, um, an escort to the dance …"

Just then, Leona Riley, Clayton and Spencer's mother, burst through the mercantile's doors. "She's here!"

Charlotte spun around as Mrs. Riley grabbed the counter to catch her breath. "Land sakes, I got the date wrong! She's arriving now, this very minute!"

Mrs. Quinn gasped in delight and clapped her hands together. "Oh, Leona, how exciting!" She turned to Matthew and hugged him. He grunted as she crushed him to her chest, and looked at Charlotte, but she was equally confused.

"Just think, another wedding!" Mrs. Riley said gaily.

"Wedding?" Charlotte squeaked. "Whose wedding?"

Matthew managed to peel his mother off him. "Yes, who's getting married now?"

The matrons faced him, both with equally enormous grins. "You are!" they said in perfect unison.

Matthew took a step back, his face paling. "What?!"

"Now before you go getting upset, hear your mother out, dear," Mrs. Riley advised.

Matthew grabbed the counter, if for nothing else than to squelch the sudden urge to wring his mother's neck. "Mother, what have you done?"

"Matthew, you know I love you. And after all, things worked out so well for Clayton and Spencer …"

Charlotte gasped. "You got Matthew a *mail-order bride*?"

Mrs. Quinn turned to her. "This is none of your business, Charlotte."

Charlotte's mouth opened in shock. "Excuse me? In about ten minutes the whole town will know."

"Only if you go around telling everyone!" she snapped back.

"Mother, I'll ask you not talk to Charlotte that way," Matthew interjected.

"Matthew, you stay out of this," his mother said as she waved him away.

"Stay out of it? Mother, you ordered me a mail-order bride without even telling me! How exactly am I supposed to stay out of that?" He glanced at Charlotte, who now looked like she was going to be quite ill.

"Well, um …" a flabbergasted Charlotte turned to Matthew. "I'd like my purchases, please," she said in a shaky voice.

He gathered them up and was about to hand them to her when he remembered what he was doing before Mrs. Riley had burst in. "Charlotte, may I …" He looked his mother right in the eye before turning back to her. "May I escort you to the Valentine's dance?"

"Matthew!" his mother barked. "You are *not* taking that … that … I got you a mail-order bride!"

"So I heard. Just now," he retorted.

Mrs. Quinn turned to her friend. "Leona! Do something!"

"Oh dear – my boys didn't make such a

fuss!" She stopped and thought for a moment. "Well, actually, they did … but they understood what drives a mother to do these things."

"With all respect, Mother, have you gone out of your mind?" Matthew's voice cracked on the word *mind*, which made him wonder. Did his mother and Mrs. Riley not think he had one? "I appreciate the thought, but you just can't go ordering brides without at least consulting the potential groom!"

"Matthew dear," Mrs. Riley said soothingly, "you might be upset now, but it'll all come out right in the end. Why, by the time you're married, I'm sure you'll be head over heels in love!"

Matthew was speechless. Had he left Boston only to come back to an insane asylum?

Charlotte was slowly backing toward the door, packages in arms.

"Matthew, what was I supposed to do?" Mrs. Quinn pleaded. "It's not like this town has any decent women left in it *to* marry!"

Matthew saw the look on Charlotte's face when she said that. "Mother!" he declared, scandalized.

Mrs. Quinn was realizing she'd overplayed her hand. "I … I didn't mean …"

"No, I'm sure you did mean it," Charlotte said. "I know what you think of me, Mrs. Quinn." She headed out the door.

"Wait!" Matthew called after her. He ran out from behind the counter, out the door, and caught up to her on the mercantile porch. "Charlotte, I don't know what's gotten into my mother ..."

"No, you don't." She looked up at him, her eyes full of regret. "You've been away a long time, Matthew. Your mother's right."

Matthew stared at her in disbelief. "I-I don't understand."

"Every town has their harpy, Matthew," she told him. "And it looks like I'm the harpy of Nowhere."

"Now I don't believe that for a moment!" Matthew argued. "And I want you to go to the dance with me!"

Charlotte's face lit up.

Mrs. Quinn stuck her head out the mercantile door. "Matthew, I don't want you to–"

Matthew didn't let her finish. "Mother, enough!" he said, looking over his shoulder at her. "I love you, and I know you want what's best for me, but I am an adult, capable of managing my own affairs – including picking out my own bride! I don't care who this woman is you thought I needed, but you sent for her, so she's your problem, not mine!"

The door to the mercantile closed with a loud thud.

Matthew turned back to Charlotte, only to see another girl standing there as well, holding a satchel in her hand. She swallowed hard and gave Matthew a tentative smile, understandable after witnessing such a tirade. "Mr. ... Mr. Matthew Quinn, I presume?"

Matthew blinked, blinked again. "Um, yes?" She was pretty; he couldn't help noticing that as she shivered at the bottom of the steps. But she wasn't as pretty as Charlotte. And was she shaking from the cold, or his anger?

"I'm Sequ … Rose. Rose Smith. Your mail-order bride."

He froze. *What a mess,* he thought.

Charlotte looked at the girl, then glanced at Matthew. "It appears you won't be escorting me after all, Matthew," she said in a tiny voice. With that, she walked down the steps, said, "Welcome to Nowhere, Miss Smith," and headed down the street – and quite possibly out of Matthew's life, forever.

ABOUT THE AUTHOR

Kit Morgan, aka Geralyn Beauchamp loves a good Western. Her father loved them as well, and they watched their fair share together over the years. To find upcoming release information and other fun news about Kit Morgan's books, check out website at :

www.authorkitmorgan.com

CPSIA information can be obtained
at www.ICGtesting.com
Printed in the USA
LVOW07s0254120118
562823LV00005B/321/P